Paris Street Tales

Paris
Street
Tales

Stories edited and
translated by

Helen Constantine

OXFORD
UNIVERSITY PRESS

OXFORD
UNIVERSITY PRESS

Great Clarendon Street, Oxford, OX2 6DP,
United Kingdom

Oxford University Press is a department of the University of Oxford.
It furthers the University's objective of excellence in research, scholarship,
and education by publishing worldwide. Oxford is a registered trade mark of
Oxford University Press in the UK and in certain other countries

First Edition published in 2016

Impression: 1

Published in the United States of America by Oxford University Press
198 Madison Avenue, New York, NY 10016, United States of America

British Library Cataloguing in Publication Data
Data available

Library of Congress Control Number: 2016940782

ISBN 978–0–19–873679–0

Printed in Great Britain by
Clays Ltd, St Ives plc

Contents

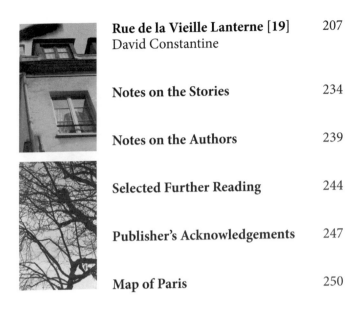

Picture Credits

Introduction

The streets of Paris are teeming with stories, as I discovered when I began compiling this book: stories of murder, adultery, and prostitution, attacks by gangsters and by pigeons, as well as somewhat less violent activities such as cycling, browsing for antiques or pondering the meaning of life. All this takes place in streets which may be variously called *rues*, *avenues*, *passages*, *impasses*, *boulevards*, *promenades*, *quais*. In the interests of variety, vital to any anthology, I have tried to include stories from different centuries, different areas of Paris, with different subjects and tones of voice; some stories are serious, some amusing. They are arranged with variety in mind, and not chronologically.

My starting point for finding out about streets in Paris was to look up their names in the remarkable books of Jacques Hillairet, who devoted his life to the study of their origins and history. He gives a detailed description of the streets, their buildings, and inhabitants, accompanied by engravings or photos of what they have looked like at various stages in their development. A list of other useful books on the history of the streets of Paris can be found at the end of this volume.

My second and equally important source of information, though not always totally reliable, was, of course, the internet, the purveyor of all sorts of surprising facts. Did you know, for instance, that of the hundreds of streets in Paris, a hundred are named after mathematicians? Wikipedia will tell you the name of the longest, shortest, narrowest, widest street in the capital. And, as with Hillairet, a little research reveals the extraordinary and bizarre stories which lie beneath the cobbles. The Rue du Chat qui Pêche, for instance, the Street of the Fishing Cat, beloved of tourists, near Saint-Michel and the Seine, is also the narrowest street in Paris, being just under two metres wide. The story goes that one Dom Perlet, a canon who dabbled in alchemy, had a black cat who could catch fish from the river with one swipe of its paw. Believing that the canon and his cat were embodiments of the devil, some students from the university nearby, or so the story goes, killed the cat, whereupon the canon vanished too. Mysteriously, almost giving credence to the students' suspicions, some time later both cat and canon reappeared in the street. For a while there was a street-art illustration of this legend on the wall. Another, grislier, story is associated with the Rue Chanoinesse in the neighbourhood of Notre-Dame. In 1387 in this street there were two shops side by side, a barber's and a pastrymaker's. The latter made pies prepared with human flesh provided by the barber, who must have been the forerunner of London's own demon barber, Sweeney Todd. According to a chronicle of 1612, the two criminals were condemned to death and burned alive on the site of their two shops.

Street names have often been the inspiration for songs as well as tales. The Rue des Blancs Manteaux is a street that belies its innocent-sounding name, immortalized in the song written by Sartre and sung by the incomparable Juliette Greco. The white robes, the 'blancs manteaux' of the title, were those of the nuns in the convent in that street, but the song is in fact all about the executions that took place there during the French Revolution:

> *Dans la rue des Blancs Manteaux*
> *Le bourreau s'est levé tôt…*

The three streets I have just referred to do not figure in the anthology, but the shortest street in Paris, the Rue des Degrés, does. This detective story by Didier Daeninckx is rooted in the twenty-first century: a body is discovered sprawled across the steps (the 'Degrés') and leads to the unravelling of a complex highly-technological criminal scam, inspired by the 9/11 attacks. The other detective story in the anthology features Simenon's Maigret and is about a murder in the Boulevard Beaumarchais, a stone's throw from the *Charlie Hebdo* offices and the massacre there in January 2015.

The fascinating names of these streets often hold the key to their history. Many are named after battles, generals, politicians, or other celebrities—poets, painters, musicians. But several hark back to a time when various trades and guilds were functioning in that particular area. In this volume the story called 'Rue de la Tacherie', by Arnaud Baignot, takes place partly in a street once noted for shops selling leather belts and other goods used for attaching objects. 'Tacherie' is an abbreviation of 'Attacherie'. Another example among many, though not in this book, is the Rue de la Verrerie in the 4th *arrondissement*, which was the focal point for the glass-making industry in the Middle Ages.

Historically the man who most influenced the development of Parisian streets was without doubt Georges-Eugène Haussmann (1809–91). Later taking the title of Baron, he was chosen by Napoleon III to carry out the massive programme of creating boulevards that dominated the nineteenth century in Paris, which from 1853 to 1870 resembled an enormous building site. We tend to think of building sites as a modern blight on the landscape but Haussmann's was the largest ever public-works project undertaken in Europe. Eighty kilometres of new avenues were cut through the old city; he had hundreds of old and insanitary buildings razed to the ground and passed a law that new ones had to be all of the same height. You do not have to go very far after arriving at the Gare du Nord (itself a creation of Haussmann) to see the result of this huge enterprise, in which one in five of the working men at the time was involved. Hundreds of pipes were laid and fresh water was brought into what had now become, with the expansion of the city into the *faubourgs*, twenty instead of twelve *arrondissements*. The Opéra Garnier was built; the market of Les Halles was completed; parks and gardens, including the Bois de Boulogne, were created. Scenes from contemporary life which illustrate the new layout of Paris streets during these decades of the middle and late nineteenth century can be seen frequently in the work of Pissarro, Renoir, and other Impressionist painters.

As with many innovatory programmes, Haussmann's inevitably meant that a large number of the little streets which had dated from medieval times and once character-ized the capital were forced to go. Baudelaire was not the only writer to regret the changing face of Paris, and reflect the unease which a transition of this kind brought about:

> *Le vieux Paris n'est plus (la forme d'une ville*
> *Change plus vite, hélas! que le cœur d'un mortel)…*

However, the lot of the poor Parisians who had to live in those conditions improved considerably after Haussmann's reforms.

One of the narrow medieval streets that was erased at that time was the Rue de la Vieille Lanterne, where the poet Gérard de Nerval, after wandering the streets, in his madness hanged himself one snowy winter's night. 'That same year the Rue de la Vieille Lanterne and all its foul connections, the leprous habitations, the cloaca, the slurried public square, the places of butchery and flaying, all were obliterated.' He did not live to see the new building created on that site, what is now the Théâtre de la Ville. The quotation comes from the only story in this anthology which was commissioned, not translated. It is an imaginative fiction, based on fact, of the poet's last weeks and his untimely end.

In their accounts of streets and the way they have changed, writers often show some nostalgia: we see it here in the pieces by Huysmans, Roland Dorgelès, and Julien Green. Huysmans, born in 1848, who presumably agreed with those who criticized Haussmann's reforms, talks about his 'tedious symmetry and banal straight lines' and contrasts with them the Rue de la Chine, which 'has preserved the appealing aspect of a country lane'. I recently went there myself and saw the towering Hôpital Tenon he describes in his essay; I also observed Asian restaurants and an oriental athlete doing Tai Chi in the pleasant Edmond Vaillant Park opposite; but alas, the street could no longer be compared to a country lane. Some fifty years later, Julien Green is also nostalgic for the past when, in his book entitled simply *Paris*, he recalls in his short piece 'Cris perdus' the lost 'cries' of Paris, in particular that of a woman who used to sell chickweed to feed the birds. There were about fifty different cries on the streets of Paris from medieval times onwards, and we have woodcuts depicting them from the beginning of the sixteenth century. The cries of chimney-sweeps, chestnut-vendors, basket-sellers, and many more could be heard in street markets throughout the capital, and the disappearance of their cries on the streets of Paris was no doubt for Green, and others, a matter of keen regret.

Roland Dorgelès (1885–1973), a writer probably not well known to English readers, is nostalgic too. In his essay 'Rooftop over the Champs-Élysées' he fondly remembers his days in Montmartre, where the 'provincial character was much to my liking' and where he lived before buying his apartment on the Champs-Élysées in what he calls the 'island of the bourgeoisie'. In Montmartre the friends he met at *Le Lapin Agile* were from the bohemian society of the time and included Francis Carco, a writer who may also be unfamiliar to English readers and whose real name was François Carcopino-Tusoli. Of Corsican origin, born in La Nouvelle-Calédonie, the French overseas territory in the South-West Pacific (annexed by Napoleon in 1854), he went to live in Paris in 1910 at the age of twenty-three, met and mingled with the artistic society of the day, and during this time had an affair with Katherine Mansfield. He writes compassionately about the lives of prostitutes and is largely known for his accounts and anecdotes of the seamier side of life in the Paris streets, which are often told in the local Parisian argot. Dorgelès refers to him as living in *une brume de mélancolie* ('a mist of melancholy').

These two writers may not be familiar to readers, but in this book there are also stories by writers who certainly will be well known: Colette, Zola, Marcel Aymé, Maupassant. All the stories I have chosen are characteristic of their particular styles and tones. With her inimitable vivacity Colette captures the atmosphere of being caught in the street crush near the Rue Ordener, where there was a famous gangster hold-up in 1911 by the Bonnot gang, a band of anarchists, and where for the first time an automobile, a Delaunay-Belleville, was used in the getaway. Zola's story takes place by the Seine—the Quai Saint-Paul near the old port which he walks along no longer exists under that name but is known today as the Quai des Célestins—where he describes a visit to a strange antique dealer's shop selling old iron objects retrieved from the waters of the Seine. One of the longer stories, Rue Saint-Sulpice, is by Marcel Aymé, who, as usual, portrays the more bizarre aspects of human behaviour with authority and is funny and sad in equal measure. The Maupassant story about a *femme du monde* evokes for us a very telling picture of upper bourgeois society at the end of the nineteenth century, which the author satirizes with his habitual skill. The writers Frédéric Fajardie, Vincent Ravalec, and, of course, Jacques Réda will also be well-known names, and I have chosen stories by these writers here, as in the other anthologies in this series set in Paris.

One thing that struck me as I read and translated these stories was how they reflected our concerns in the twenty-first century. This was so not only in the more overtly modern stories, like Aurélie Filippetti's account of conversations about immigrants in a café, or Ravalec's Beckett-like characters pondering the subject of AIDS and mad-cow disease, but also in the social hypocrisy inherent in Maupassant's 'Le Rendez-vous' or the fierce debate about the freedom of the individual in Octave Mirbeau's 'conte cruel'.

I hope every reader will find something to enjoy in these stories, and that they will add to the interest of those who, as I do, like reading about, as well as wandering through, the streets of this great capital.

* * *

Since translating these stories and writing this introduction, unspeakable events have taken place in the streets of Paris—the attacks on the satirical magazine *Charlie Hebdo*, and the massacre of young people in the Bataclan theatre, amongst others. This book is therefore dedicated to their memory and to the brave Parisians who, in spite of the threats of barbarians, daily assert their right to walk in freedom in the streets of their city.

Rue des Degrés

Didier Daeninckx

Not very far from the former Cour des Miracles, separated only by a narrow row of ancient houses above dressmakers' shops and clothes outlets, the Rue de Cléry and the Rue Beauregard almost converge. The clicking of sewing machines mingles with the hum of traffic, the shouts of trolley-pushers, the cries of people carrying clothes, the cursing of drivers whose way is blocked on the tarmac by endless deliveries. Women's eyes gleam from shadowy entrances, their low-cut dresses ogled by men hesitating behind their beers. Just before they join the Grands Boulevards, level with the Porte Saint-Denis, the twin streets are connected by the smallest street in Paris, stretching six metres at the very most, fourteen steps, which give it its name, Rue des Degrés: a street lamp, steps with two blank walls on either side, a metal handrail in the middle, polished by the rubbing of the clothes of passers-by. It was there beneath the red stencil of a punk's face and the words 'What if I look down?' that the cleaning woman from *Chez Victoria* found the body of Flavien Carvel, early one morning when she was taking out the rubbish. He was lying on his stomach across the steps and his head, covered in blood, was resting on the heap of flattened cardboard left there by the shopkeepers of the *quartier*. Brown streaks defaced the right-hand wall under the flaking paint of an Artex advertisement. When the police turned the corpse over, they saw that the blood had come from a wound in the stomach, most likely from a knife attack, soaking the hair below. While they were cordoning off a security area, one of the men, Lieutenant Mattéo, followed different traces of blood along the Rue Beauregard, as far as the *Café Mauvoisin*, whose owner was just raising his metal shutter. Over the sign, a candle was burning at the feet of a Madonna sheltered in a niche.

'Did you close late last night?'

'It was locked up at midnight...Has somebody been complaining?'

'No, the only person who could have complained can't complain any more! Was everything all right? Nothing out of the ordinary occurred?'

He fingered his moustache which he had smoothed several times, his thumb and first finger splayed.

'No, hardly anyone was here because of the football match, I've never installed a TV in the café…It's a café, not a picture palace. Two customers were sitting at the small table under the picture of La Voisin, the poisoner who lived here, or so they say…I waited for them to finish their beers before I drew down the shutters…'

The policeman went to take a look inside. It smelled of damp and stale tobacco.

'There wasn't anyone with shoulder-length fair hair, black jeans, white tennis-shoes and blouson jacket…about twenty-five…?'

'Yes there was…he sat facing me. He drank two beers, two Leffes, but he couldn't take his alcohol very well… Unless he'd had a few before he got to my place. They walked out along the pavement towards where you are now, walked away twenty yards while I was putting down the shutters. I remember they stopped and carried on talking. The young man you mentioned leaned against the wall, and the other one crossed over to the Rue de la Lune a bit farther down. I don't suppose he wanted to drag him along too. It wasn't very nice of him to leave a mate in a state like that. The chap in jeans teetered off in the direction of the Porte Saint-Denis and I went home to bed.'

Lieutenant Mattéo studied the owner of the *Mauvoisin*.

'I'm sorry but I don't think you'll be opening this morning…You'll have to come with me. Your last customer of the evening wasn't drunk: he'd just been stabbed several times in the stomach. He was found on the steps of the Rue des Degrés. The traces of blood begin at exactly the spot you showed me…'

After questioning the barman they learned that the two men had arrived one after the other in the café, Carvel first, at about eleven, then his presumed killer ten minutes later. They had been talking softly, calmly, without it being possible to grasp what the conversation was about. It was the victim who had paid for the drinks with a fifty-euro note. The second man, just as unfamiliar to the owner as the man opposite him, was about thirty, elegantly dressed, smaller than average, dark, with a round face, speaking with a very slight Spanish accent.

'He had a small port-wine stain on his temple and tried to hide it by pulling a strand of hair over it. A sort of tic…'

Almost everything they knew about Flavien Carvel they got from the identity papers found in the pockets of his blouson jacket. It stated that he was born 21 April 1982 in Antony, that he was a decorator and lived in the Impasse du Gaz at La Plaine Saint-Denis. The visas and stamps that decorated his passport indicated that in the course of the last eight months Carvel had gone to the United States, Australia, Japan, Vanuatu and Lebanon and stayed no more than a week in each. Theft did not constitute a motive for murder if you took into consideration that the murderer had not stolen his bank cards or the 800 euros in cash lining his pockets. Slipped in between the plastic rectangles of the Platinum American Express card and Visa Infinite, Mattéo discovered a piece of paper torn from the margin of a newspaper and written on in biro:

'Tom Cruise was seen last Monday in the Rue de la Paix, in the 2nd *arrondissement* in Paris, in the company of the wife of a candidate for the French Presidential election, while rumours of the separation of the American star and Katie Holmes are headlines in the popular press.'

Mattéo had gone to the Plaine Saint-Denis at the beginning of the afternoon, after eating a slice of Tuscan pizza at the *Casa della Pasta* in the Rue Montorgueil. It was years since he'd set foot in the northern *périphérique*. He remembered it as being a dreary grey, full of gasometers, the outer walls of refineries and coke works, factory chimneys, façades the colour of ash streaming with rain non-stop, the open sewer of the Autoroute du Nord and its endless stream and stink of traffic... The building of the Stade de France had utterly altered the geography of the area. The last signs of the old industrial revolution had been erased. Head offices rose as if on parade along the flowering walkways which now concealed the cloaca of traffic. The straight green hedges, as well as the wanderings of the clouds, were reflected in the brushed aluminium, the smoked glass, the polished steel. The formula which had been successful in Paris, the one which, thanks to Beaubourg, the Forum des Halles, the Opéra Bastille, the Arche de la Défense, the Grande Bibliothèque, had allowed the city to be emptied of its underclasses was being replicated nowadays in the near suburbs. A grand architectural gesture in the urban maquis: nothing like it for taking possession of Paris again! Lieutenant Mattéo had always lived in the 2nd *arrondissement*, and couldn't imagine moving from there even to an area close by. Montorgueil, Tiquetonne, Réaumur, Aboukir, Le Sentier, all those streets were like the life lines on the palm of his hand. Except that over the last ten years or so he'd had to come to terms with the mass influx of yuppies who every month spent on the café terraces of the *Rocher de Cancale*, the *Compas d'Or* or the *Loup Blanc* what the soaring rent on his flat cost him. He walked along the canal, past the camps of Romanies mixed with all the homeless who had been driven away from the banks of the Seine, then entered what remained of the old Spanish quarter by the Rue Cristino Garcia. L'Impasse du Gaz consisted of four or five red brick houses, joined together like the terraces in mining towns. A bit like England. Cranes were turning round and round just behind this surviving relic. The name Carvel, followed by the first name Mélanie, was displayed on a letter-box. It occurred to him that it was the same name as his assistant's. He pulled the chain hanging near the wire-meshed door. A woman of about fifty came and opened it, dragging her feet after crossing what was probably a passage and complaining the while. Yellow, tired-looking wavy hair from an old perm, a washed-out face, blue eyelids, the corners of her slack mouth turned down. The rest of her body looked equally worn out, Flavien's mother was the very picture of defeat, of neglect. Contrary to what the lieutenant had feared, she received the news of her son's death without breaking down. She did no more than clench her teeth and prevent her right hand from shaking before wiping away on the back of her sleeve the tears which sprang to her eyes.

'How did it happen?'

As he went in Mattéo glanced into the dining room where, in front of the television lit up like a night light, a low table was collapsing under empty bottles and ashtrays overflowing with cigarette butts.

'We don't know very much yet. His murderer could be of Spanish extraction. There are quite a lot in that area: your son must have gone around with some of them...'

'Yes, dozens. At one time he used to go nearby to the *Patronage* to play cards, dance, eat tapas...'

'"At one time", when would that be?'

She pushed back a sliding door to reveal an untidy bedroom with walls studded with posters. The tight-lipped smile of Bill Gates looked quite out of place amongst the dazzling white teeth of showbiz stars from cinema and sport.

'For two years he just blew in like a puff of wind. We must have had a meal together once or twice with his current girlfriend...Last week he brought me some flowers for my birthday...'

'Do you remember their names?'

She got out a packet of Lucky Strike from the pocket of her cardigan, lit the end of a cigarette with a Zippo which stank of butane.

'The girls' names? No. He changed girls even more often than he changed cars...I don't know what make they were either.'

Mattéo did not ask permission to go into the room. He began to search through the collection of video games, albums, films, magazines. A few lines scribbled on a notebook suddenly caught his attention:

'Sunday, 28th August, New Orleans. The storm is coming, it's getting stronger all the time. The telephone is ringing incessantly. "Are you going or staying?" "Where are you living?" "Have you got your cats with you?" "What do we have to do?" The Governor asks us to "pray that the hurricane goes down to Category 2"...I am giving in finally to the pressure. I'm going to move into a building that's more solid. A former canning factory in the town centre made of bricks and cement and five storeys high. There are seven of us in the flat with four cats.'

It was the same sloping, nervous writing as the message about Tom Cruise and the Presidential candidate's wife. He held out the paper under the nose of Flavien's mother.

'Did he write that?'

'Yes, that's his writing. He was always noting things down, always scribbling... Things he'd heard on the radio, on television, that people told him over the telephone or that he'd found in the newspapers. It was a sort of obsession, I was tired of telling him not to, but he couldn't help it.'

'Do you know where he was living latterly?'

She nodded vaguely.

'I only know he'd bought some place in Paris... He never gave me his phone number. Only his email address, but what would I do with that? I haven't even got a computer!'

The lieutenant's mobile began to vibrate in his trouser pocket. He waited until he was outside the house in the Impasse du Gaz to answer it. He took the phone away from his head hurriedly when Burdin's shrill tones began piercing his eardrums.

'I wanted to let you know that we have a lead for the body on the Rue des Degrés. He doesn't appear on the files at all, a real ghost. I've done the rounds of my informers with his photo round my neck. He hung out for a while in the back room of the *Singe Pèlerin*, the place where the

managers of the sex shops inspect their walking meat…
It seems he was interested in one of the clubs but I don't
know which one…'

Mattéo knew the informer at the *Singe Pèlerin*, a barman there, for the very good reason that he had recruited
him five years earlier, when he caught him sniffing coke.
The café, which had once been a place where they ripened
bananas, was hidden in a corner, two steps away from
where the Place du Caire begins, built over the mythical
Cour des Miracles. For decades he had never wondered
about that name, whose likely meaning had been provided
the previous week by a drunk exhibitionist who'd had to be
evicted from the Rue Saint-Sauveur to spare the blushes
of passers-by. The explanation from the sobering-up cell
at the police station had required upwards of an hour, but
could be summarized in a few words. Every evening when
the beggars who were scattered across the city went back
to their dens, pockets clinking with coins, it was as if
Christ had leaned over them: the blind could see again, the
legless cripples got to their feet, the scrofulous were rid
of their sores, the deaf could hear noises, the dumb began
to sing, Siamese-twin girls faced each other; it was enough
to go as far as the perimeter of the refuge for the miracle to
happen! The lieutenant pressed the handle and pushed
open the glass door on which there was an ancient telephone number dating from the time when letters rather

than figures were used. About thirty girls were sitting on moleskin seats waiting to be assessed in the room at the back. They were mostly girls from Eastern Europe or Africa, one Asian and one Indian. He made straight for the bar, leaned on it in front of his nark and, hardly opening his mouth, gave his orders.

'A strong black coffee and get over to the usual place right away…'

The barman began to protest, but Mattéo had already turned round to admire the tapering legs of an Estonian girl who was passing the time by pulling pink chewing-gum from her silicone lips. He made a face as he swallowed his unsweetened arabica, crossed the room, went up the Rue Saint-Denis thirty metres and vanished into the shop of the last straw-hat maker in the Place de Paris. Assaf, the boss, had been born on the first floor of the shop. Rounded up by the French police, like all the Jews in the area, he had survived the inferno of Auschwitz before making a ten-year detour through the camps of his liberators. Good relations between the lieutenant and the hat maker had been established when Mattéo had got rid of a band of racketeers. After that he had got into the habit of coming to play chess with the old man, who hardly ever talked about his past unless it was to go over the games, which he had always lost, where he had played against a champion from Soviet Russia suspected of Trotskyist leanings. Tournaments being forbidden by the administration of the Gulag, one prisoner had had a chessboard tattooed on his back. He would go down on all fours the time it took for a player to be checkmated. Mattéo put his arms round his old friend.

'You are going to have a visit from a client. But don't get excited, I can tell you now he won't buy anything...You can go into the kitchen, I'll bring him along as soon as he shows up.'

The barman from the *Singe Pèlerin* had donned a raincoat over his work outfit. He asked for some water to swallow a handful of pills, refused the seat that the lieutenant pointed him to.

'I can't stay, there's a sudden rush on. All the big boys are there. What do you want with me? Is it about the chap who got shot on the Rue des Degrés?'

'If you ask the questions and tell me the answers it'll be quicker...His name was Flavien Carvel and he wasn't shot, he was knifed...What do you know about him?'

The barman raised his head, his mouth open as though searching for fresh air.

'The only thing I know is that he was loaded. He began coming round here about six months ago. He took out shares in the *Sphinx*, as a way of getting to know those people. Lately it was said he was buying a huge share in the peepshow on the corner of the Rue Greneta...Top class stuff. They were saying it must have cost him 200,000 euros to get his way in.'

'I was involved with that two years ago. It was real cut-throat stuff. Are you sure you've got the right place?'

Mattéo got up to fill a pan with water and set it to boil on the gas.

'No, they got it all back on track. It's one of the clubs that make the most money. All the income circulates in cash, tax-free, seeing that the clients aren't the kind to leave their address before they go into the cabins! As far as I know there were quite a few extras...'

'What sort of extras?'

'They opened up little trap doors through which the client could paw the breasts and bottoms of the dancers, and stick dildos or vibrators in them, back and front. Stuff that you could only buy in the shop at top price...If the client wanted you could do it the other way, the dancers brought them off with the help of the same tools.'

'Have you any idea where he lived?'

The barman thrust his hand into a pocket in his rain-coat, took out a visiting card and held it out to the police-man.

'I did him a favour by telling him about the things I heard...He told me that I could contact him via this estate agent's in an emergency...'

Mattéo took from him the card of LuxImmo, an establishment in the Rue Marie-Stuart. He memorized the name printed under the company name, Tristanne Dupré, then automatically turned the card over. The back was covered with Carvel's nervous handwriting:

'26 December might have been the best day of Rafiq's life, if the tsunami had not struck, since he was supposed to get married on that day. The time of his wedding was fixed for midday but the waves arrived in the course of the morning. Rafiq was in the village of Parangipettai, near other villages affected. Immediately all the men in the community got organized under the Jamaat banner, their local organization. They took all the food prepared for the wedding and went and gave it to the victims. Until the day we met them one week after the tsunami it provided food for the breakfast and lunch of the people affected (rice cooked in lemon or vegetable biryani).'

He drank fresh mint tea sweetened with acacia honey before taking his leave of old Assaf. You only had to move a hundred metres and the second-hand clothes and sex shops disappeared, you entered the domain that had passed to people who had made their money from the new economic deal. All the darlings from the world of finance, advertising, high office and the media were out walking on the inoffensive pavements, well kitted out, good to look at. There was a crush on the terraces where you paid a hefty toll to sip a vitamin cocktail through a fluorescent straw, mobile jammed to your ear. In spite of all this, Mattéo liked the place: the façades, the smell of the eternal city;

but he had lived there too long in the old days not to realize the vacuousness of it all. Crossing from the Rue Saint-
Denis to the Rue Montorgueil was like crossing a frontier.
He felt a little as though he was in a theatre, almost a tour-
ist. He was sorry he had not slung his camera round his
neck. He quickened his pace. Tramps were sorting through
the bins lined up outside the *Soguisa*, *La Fermette*, *Furusato*,
the Japanese restaurant, looking for food waste from the
health-food shop. He branched off into the Rue Marie-
Stuart, which used to be in fierce competition with the Rue
Brisemiche in the old days when it was called, more prosaically, Passage Tire-Vit and, later, Tire-Boudin. The estate
agent occupied the ground floor of an old bare-stone house
with exposed wooden beams, heart of oak. Tristanne Dupré
resembled the girls in the waiting-room of the *Singe Pèlerin*.
The way she was upholstered may have been exactly the
same but the number plate could not have been more different. Everything about her, from her stockings to her
haircut, from her court shoes to her perfume, came straight
out of the pages of *Vogue*. Her skirt was a Badgley Mishka,
her shoes Alexander McQueen, her glasses Caroline Herrera…
At a glance you could calculate how much had been spent
on each item. Mattéo slipped the card on to the desk—he
had seen one like it in Beaubourg.

'According to what I hear, you served as postbox for
Flavien Carvel…'

Her eyes behind the slightly smoked glasses widened before she looked the inspector up and down, disdainfully.

'I don't understand...'

'Mattéo, police. Carvel is in the morgue and I am trying to nobble the bloke who bought him the one-way ticket. Soonest would be best. You two made a team to buy back the peepshow in the Rue de Greneta, is that it?'

This possibility had risen to his lips without him even thinking about it. By her fluttering lashes he realized his attack had hit home. Now he had to withdraw the blade without further damage.

'Flavien dead? No, it can't be true!'

She threw herself back against her chair, her chest under the silk agitated by heaving breaths. Her distress was not faked. He wondered if she was one of the interchangeable girls who waited for the prodigal son in the car when he went to visit his mother in the Impasse du Gaz. He pushed away a pile of interior decoration magazines and sat on the sofa.

'Oh, I'm sorry, I didn't know you were as close as that. He was found stabbed this morning near the Porte Saint-Denis...I should like to know how you got acquainted...'

She fitted a Camel cigarette into a snakeskin holder and lit it with the matching lighter.

'In the simplest possible way. He pushed open this door and sat down exactly in the place you are sitting...He was trying to buy a flat in the pedestrian zone, with a preference for Tiquetonne...After dozens of visits he had decided on a large four-room apartment in a listed building in the Rue Léopold-Bellan...

'Expensive in that area. Did you give him a price?'

She shrugged.

'Seven thousand euros per square metre. It was about one hundred and twenty...I'll let you do the multiplication...Flavien had a third of that sum, he was hoping to cover the rest through revenues from the peepshow. He was going to fit the place out next month.'

'Where was he living in the meantime?'

'Up above here on the third floor in a studio flat, in the same building as this shop...I've got a spare set of keys.'

Mattéo also learned that the agency was the owner of the building containing the rooms for the voyeurs, that it was Tristanne who had put her moneyed client on to it, and that his bank was on the Place de la Bourse near the premises of the *Nouvel Observateur*. As he was getting ready to climb up to the third floor, he suddenly returned to the desk. He turned over the visiting card to reveal the notes Flavien had written.

'Do you know why he used to write bits of newspaper items on all the paper he got hold of?'

'No, he copied them on to his computer in the evening to provide material for his website, that's all he told me...I kept several...I remember that he made a copy of all his work on his USB.'

The young woman opened her bag, a Vuitton, and rummaged.

'Here, this is him...'

The policeman examined the piece of paper:

'Since the beginning of the riots, the police are jumpier, they are pushing us more and more. The brother of one of the children electrocuted was with us as usual at the bottom of his block of flats when the police arrived with their thunderflashes. They stared at us and then said to him: "You get home to your Mum." He took three paces towards the cops to speak to them, one of them said to him: "Stop or you'll burn." We escaped up to the tenth floor, they began shooting tear gas into the hall. They filled the flat—and the grieving family in there—with smoke.'

He had just finished reading when she passed him another:

'Cotonou airport, 25 December. I had a very bad feeling and I was very ill at ease. Each time something bad is going to happen to me, I know it. And in this case my sixth sense told me we were not going to take off. I was truly expecting something to happen. I even told one of my colleagues about my feeling. A few moments later we were still in the plane but in the water. The people who were still alive were panicking and screaming. I wasn't afraid because

I had felt that something awful was about to happen. Everything happened very quickly. I should think it was only two minutes from take-off to the accident. From the place I got out of the aeroplane, I was not far from the shore. So I swam to get back to land and to save my life.'

He put them in his wallet with the previous ones and made his way to the stairs. He did not need to use the bunch of keys provided by the estate agent. The door had been forced, every single corner of the flat thoroughly gone through. The lieutenant contemplated the ruin, the pulled-out drawers, the bed turned upside down and the mattress slit open. He lifted the furniture looking for the computer, the memory stick Tristanne had just mentioned. The visitor had taken everything, it seemed. The only scrap judged insignificant was a last enigmatic message thrown into the waste-paper basket in the bathroom: 'On 26 December Rababa and his son Hamed were asleep when the earthquake shook the small town of Bam in Iran. Before they even had time to run outside their house collapsed around them. They remained imprisoned for four days until a neighbour came to rescue them, scooping out the rubble with his bare hands.'

He walked back up as far as the Rue de la Lune near the old postern gate of La Poissonnerie, where the tide had once come into Paris at dawn. It was a tiny, almost provincial enclave with its square, its church, its groups of children, yet only two steps away from the ceaseless flow of the Grands Boulevards, the excitement of the Rue Saint-Denis, the preserve of the bourgeoisie. From his kitchen he could see the ceramic sign of the Castrique buildings which promised 'cleaning by suction'. He had kept his flat after the divorce, after Annabelle and the kids had left, devoting almost half his income to renting a place where he used only two rooms out of four. Everything was ready for them to move back in. To go somewhere else would have been to admit defeat. He heated up a tagine, chicken with lemon and carrots cooked by the Moroccan concierge who also did his washing and housework. Later he watched a detective film on television, just as if he were seeing the landscape go by from out of a train window—unable to follow the plot, his mind completely occupied with the murder of Flavien Carvel. The next morning, having called in at the police station, Mattéo appeared at the director's office of the Financière des Victoires, the bank which managed Carvel's accounts. Nobody seemed to be aware of the loss of an important client the night before in the Rue des Degrés. The missing man's personal adviser consented very ungraciously to enter into his computer the secret code which allowed access to information about the transfer of funds.

'The net amount in Monsieur Carvel's account is nearly 400,000 euros. Also we have guaranteed transactions for twice that sum. Building projects. I can draw up a state-ment to the nearest centime.'

'Thank you, but what would be really useful to me is to know where Flavien Carvel drew his income from... I understand his fortune materialized rather suddenly. One might wonder how... Was it all legal, so far as you can judge?'

The adviser's neck stiffened at the suggestion of money-laundering.

'I don't know why you should suspect any such thing...'

'No reason... perhaps just experience... I am only asking for reassurance. Where did these 400,000 euros come from?'

He turned the screen towards the lieutenant and scrolled through the dozens of pages.

'From all over the place... Europe, the States, Japan, Russia, South Africa. A hundred countries altogether... Last month he received nearly 10,000 payments by inter-net with an average of three euros for each transaction. He sold connection times, access to information...'

Mattéo took his wallet from his pocket and unfolded the torn piece of paper he had found on the body.

'This kind of thing?'

The banker took it gingerly and read the message:

'Tom Cruise was seen last Monday in the Rue de la Paix, in the 2nd *arrondissement* in Paris, in the company of the wife of a candidate for the French Presidential election, while rumours of the separation of the American star and Katie Holmes are headlines in the popular press.'

'Our job is limited to verifying that transactions conform with the law, to regulate the flow as best as we can in the common interest of the bank and its clients. We forbid the slightest intervention in the activities of the latter. All I can tell you is that Monsieur Carvel drew his income from selling information on the web. That's all. I shall make copies of these available to the magistrate.'

'We'll wait...'

When he left, a group of people had gathered in the Rue Notre-Dame-des-Victoires. A banner in the colours of the rainbow secured to the railings of the Bourse announced the erection of the 'Cursed Stone'. He mingled with the onlookers to witness the inauguration of a sort of monument in the shape of a coffin which bore the names of all the present-day dictators or war criminals. He moved away when the police car sirens sounded. His steps took him to the rag-trade quarter. As he went up the Rue Beauregard again he saw the moustachioed boss of the *Café Mauvoisin* polishing his percolator in the dark interior, then he slowly retraced the final journey of Flavien Carvel up to the fourteen steps of the Rue des Degrés. The Highways Department had erased the traces of the murder. All that survived was the memory of the bloody body rubbing against that blank wall beneath the enamelled advertisement of the Artex firm. The lieutenant went over and stood hugging the wall as though exactly in the position of the victim. He raised his eyes and then noticed a few drops of blood thirty centimetres above his head. He heaved himself up on tiptoe and ascertained that there were still more a little higher up on the edge of the plaque where it said 'Artex distributor of Chaldée Créations'. He slid the tip of his finger under the bottom right-hand corner, which was slightly raised, and jiggled it around. A tiny object freed from the pressure of the metal fell at his feet. He bent down and picked up the memory stick which Flavien had just managed to hide before he died. Ten minutes later, Mattéo was installing the contents of the disk on to his computer. Two icons representing videos appeared in the middle of other files. The first was titled: '11-09-01', the second: 'Tom-Cécilia'. He double-clicked on the latter. The scientologist actor and the errant wife were walking and laughing near the Opéra in Paris before entering the *Café de la Paix*, arm in arm. Innocuous pictures that only a tendentious commentator could transform into a secret idyll. The second sequence, which also lasted one minute, was in a completely different tone. It was visibly filmed by a surveillance camera equipped with zoom placed on top of a building forming a terrace, of which you could see one corner of the façade when the lens scanned across it. Opposite, you could recognize the massive architecture of the Pentagon and in front of it gardens, carparks, approach roads dotted with sentry-boxes, for security. After about fifteen seconds of the web-cam's slow tracking, a white object pierced the field of vision from the right, crossed the picture, hit one of the sections of the concrete wall and was swallowed up, as though it had been absorbed by a huge sheaf of flames. A digital display told the date and hour of the crash: '09-11/9.43 a.m.' In the slow motion which followed, you could recognize the fuselage of a Boeing 757 in the colours of American Airlines. It was just as evident, as frightening, as the news clips showing the approach of the two planes which were about to hit the Twin Towers. Mattéo could not remember having seen a film that was so clear as this of the attack on the American Ministry of Defence in Arlington. Everything that the administration of President Bush had offered the public to counter the conspiracy theories did not hold water but here before Mattéo's eyes was the reality of the explosion of Flight AA77 as clear as daylight. He opened the other files, which contained several dozen texts similar to those he had come across in his investigation into Flavien Carvel, documents of all the plagues that had hit the planet in the course of the last months: tsunamis, earthquakes, deadly pollution, suicide bombings, cyclones, volcanic eruptions…Each extract accompanied by its origin, a name, first name, telephone contact number or internet address, with a sum made out in euros attached. The panicky escape of a group of tourists from an fiery inferno in the Philippines had a price tag of 300 euros, the confession of a child martyr from Hezbollah with a belt packed with explosives rated 200 euros, whereas the image of an old man being carried off by a giant wave in Thailand was worth 1,000. Only one paragraph was without its valuation, the one which had to do with the circumstances of the destruction of the exterior rings of the Pentagon. On the other hand, the details of the presumed source of the document were there: Fidel Hernandez. That could be a match for the elegant fellow who spoke with the slight Spanish accent in the *Café Mauvoisin* in the Rue Beauregard, in the company of Flavien Carvel, just before he was stabbed near the Rue des Degrés. Mattéo's assistant needed barely two hours to obtain the address provided by Hernandez for his telephone account, a hotel situated near the Bourse.

'It seems to be the real thing. I've been able to verify the activity of his mobile in the course of the last three days: several of his calls were relayed by the local transmitters.'

'Thanks, Mélanie...'

Mattéo went round the Palais Brongniart before going back up to the Bibliothèque Nationale. The Royal Richelieu, jammed in between two banks, displayed its gilded interlaced initials beneath the six storeys of a Haussmann building. The detective went in and leaned on the reception desk.

'Good morning. I'd like to speak to Monsieur Fidel Hernandez…I don't know his room number.'

The receptionist consulted the screen for reservations.

'I'm sorry but there's nobody of that name…'

'He was here yesterday, I'm told…'

She played with her keyboard, consulted several pages of records.

'No, there's been no Hernandez in recent weeks…None.'

Mattéo slid his card on to the polished wood.

'I can't explain, but it's very important…This Hernandez perhaps stayed here under another name. Very dapper, quite small, round-faced, a touch of a Spanish accent…'

The receptionist's shrug was accompanied by a pout that showed her dimples.

'I can't think who…'

Mattéo pointed to his own temple with his forefinger.

'He has a port-wine spot there and he constantly tries to hide it by pulling his hair over it…'

The young woman's face lit up with a smile.

'That's not Monsieur Hernandez, that's Monsieur Herrera! You have the wrong name! He's been with us for a week. Room 227 on the second floor. Do you want me to call him?'

He laid a hand on hers as she was beginning to pick up the phone.

'Absolutely not. Give me the other key to his room, I'm going to give him a surprise…'

When he got to the landing, the lieutenant took his revolver out of his belt before putting the key in the lock. Hernandez, stretched out naked on the bed watching a pay-channel film, started when he heard the click. Against all Mattéo's expectations, he put his hands over his private parts instead of trying to grab a gun. Opening his box in the hotel safe allowed Mattéo to recover the computer and the memory stick stolen from the temporary apartment of Flavien Carvel above the office of Tristanne Dupré. Fidel Hernandez was not called Herrera either, but Miguel Cordez. Originally from Mexico, he had been living in France for about ten years, making a very good living meddling in fraud, each affair more ingenious than the one before. The development of sites offering amateur pay-videos like Flickr, Dailymotion, Starbucks and YouTube had caught his attention. Operations that were too big for him. He had thrown in his lot with a small new one called Newscoop, created a few months earlier by Carvel.

'I knew quite a few of the members of the team. As soon as there was a disaster somewhere, I went to Roissy or New York to get the photos or films from the first people who were coming back from there… I managed to buy exclusives for almost nothing on the tsunami, on Katrina…'

'Where did the film of the surveillance camera on the Pentagon come from?'

Miguel Cordez raised his right hand to his forehead.

'A cousin of mine works in security in Washington... He pirated it before the services could gather all the stuff together and place an embargo on it. He was asking 100,000 dollars. Carvel agreed straight away, but I learned that he was making underhand negotiations to sell it on for six times the price...'

'So that's what you were discussing, at the *Mauvoisin*? He didn't want to give in, or give you back the recording...'

'That's right.'

That evening a special adviser from the Ministère des Affaires Étrangères came and took the video showing the impact of Flight AA77 on the Pentagon so that it could be given back to the American authorities. The only thing Lieutenant Mattéo was still wondering was what the alcoholic from the Impasse du Gaz would do with all the money she'd inherit from her son.

Streets

Jean Follain

A house with the façade painted yellow, in the sunshine, a dejected-looking woman with her head bowed at a window.

A policeman and some navvies are standing around in the street. The red wine from the vineyards of Le Hérault and Algeria flows in the wine-shops, where serving girls, perspiring a little, laugh, sponge oilcloths and polish the splendid zinc at the bar.

The solitary tree in the Parisian courtyard is bedecked with Île-de-France green, blending with the most sumptuous grey.

Conversations come at us from all sides. Vulgarities give you such a strong feeling of life that you feel like hugging the women who utter them, on the street and in their homes as well, beside their little polished stoves. In the air human smells mix with those smells of vinegar, onions, frying; they issue from open windows, windows which look out on to the Sacré-Cœur, Notre-Dame or a graveyard.

Every day you can transcribe on to the harsh slate of everyday life a marvellous *Carte de Tendre*. You would have to include on it the painted rose above the door of a brothel in Grenelle in the midday sun, the obscure graffiti on the wall of a local church built in the Second Empire, the gesture of a street urchin who, as though to pluck a delicious moment from the air, with fingers splayed, spreads out the palm of his grubby little hand on the burning hot wall.

Desolate walkers peer at saucy postcards, the soles of their shoes are wearing out. Cold or hot rain made large holes in them as big as royal *écus*.

In the newly-green squares mothers open their corsages to nurse their babies, a small piece of silver braid shines on the collar of the park keeper's tunic. In the grocers' shops the assistants fill grey sacks with rock salt. In the doorway of her dairy a woman sucks the blood from a small cut on her finger. Locksmiths are cutting and filing keys. The tripe sellers display their calves' hearts on the marble slabs.

Wide-eyed matrons and young housewives who feel the cold, their satiny skin getting worn away gradually beneath woollen garments, buy products of the chemical industry from the hardware shop: bleach, cats' head soap and soap veined red and blue... On café terraces a dash of syrup makes a fleetingly delicate cloud in the sparkling aperitif, a glass smashes, a child cries.

Silence fills a whole street, on which, through a window, you can see a girl with a naked back washing herself.

It happens that you sometimes walk along streets without any charm or distinction, which remain, as it were, abstracted, where night comes down more simply, where the hours chime more clearly, streets which are suddenly made famous by a mysterious murder.

In some of them, with turn-of-the-century façades, adorned with identical balconies, in rooms decorated in garish colours melancholic couples give themselves up to the pleasures of the flesh amid the faded furniture: the evening newspaper is opened on a chair, the mice gnaw at a piece of Gruyère abandoned in a saucer. All these things are part and parcel of a night in Paris, the wind blowing as it used to blow in the old days, when the *chouans* went out reconnoitring under a starless sky.

It's good to walk back up those colourless streets with a friend and your eyes not being distracted by anything. Beneath your feet you can feel the comforting pavement, while you chat to one another, cheer yourselves up, enjoy making distinctions and clarifying things; you can scarcely hear the whistle of that passer-by, scarcely see that great hound following his preoccupied master with the same noble bearing he would have when he followed him into the autumn woods.

And it's on the pavements of these streets, beneath the illuminated cigars of the tobacco shops that are about to close, that you strengthen those loyalties you hold so dear, that you can recall once again together some splendid image, while close by two policemen discuss the exam they will have to sit for promotion; they will have to be very good at spelling, fractions, long division, though not the movement of the planets.

A man from Finistère walks along the Rue Réaumur. A smell of burnt fat emanates from the dwarf shrubs on the terrace of an eating-house which has a silver sign advertising soup. Workers buy one another noxious drinks which afford them some comfort in the time-honoured way. It's towards the Temple quarter that the Breton is making his way, he draws from his pocket a short white pipe. Jews emerge from an ochre-coloured café where they have been drinking lemon tea out of stemmed glasses, with briefcases full of gems, some hiding wounds, others escaped from shipwrecks. They are wearing grey or brown suits of a coarse cloth and they do not smoke. The quiet Breton enters the café to have a coffee. They make their way, chattering, towards the Rue des Rosiers, they are going to visit the fat woman who dozes almost all day long on an eiderdown the colour of peony from which, through holes in the silk eider, feathers float away on the caress of a foul-smelling breeze.

A horse in a lather in the July heat races down the Rue des Envierges. Children hide in concierges' lodges. The little salesgirl wearing a Berrichon headdress, wakened out of her daydreams, quakes in her shop. She was thinking about the day when strange, coloured globes appeared round the sun, and when there was that viper slithering towards the teacher who was lying on his front in the little yellow wood, completely unaware of the danger he was in.

A sergeant on leave rushes to bring the horse under control while its rider, quite unperturbed, shuffles cards in the *Café de la Vielleuse*, where, above the large mirror shattered by a shell in the war, is a painting of the woman with black ribbons playing the hurdy-gurdy.

The Rendez-vous

Guy de Maupassant

Wearing her hat and coat, one veil covering her face and another in her pocket to place over the first as soon as she was in that sinful cab, she tapped the pointed end of her little boot with the spike on her umbrella and sat in her room, unable to make up her mind whether or not to go to this rendez-vous.

And yet how many times had she got ready like this to go and meet her lover, the handsome Vicomte de Martelet, in his bachelor apartment, while her husband, very much the man of the world, was at work in the Stock Exchange?

Behind her the clock loudly ticked away the seconds; a half-read book lay open on the rosewood desk between the windows, and two bunches of violets bathing in the dainty little Meissen vases on the mantelpiece gave off a heady perfume, which mingled with the subtle scent of verbena wafting out of the half-open bathroom door.

The clock chimed—three o'clock—and made her get to her feet. She turned her head to look at the clock-face, then smiled as she thought: 'He's already waiting. He'll be getting impatient.' Whereupon she left, telling the servant she'd be back within the hour at the latest—a lie—and, going down the stairs, went out into the street.

It was nearing the end of May, that delightful time of the year when spring seems to come in from the country-side and besiege Paris, over the rooftops, invading the houses through their very walls, decking the city with flowers, rejoicing her stone façades, her pavements and even the cobbles on the streets, flooding the city and making her drunk with sap, as in a greening wood.

Madame Haggan took a few steps to the right, meaning to walk along the Rue de Provence, as she usually did, and hail a cab, but the sweetness of the air, that feeling that summer was coming—some days it almost caught you by the throat—hit her so suddenly that she changed her mind and went down the Rue de la Chaussée d'Antin, not knowing why, but vaguely drawn by a desire to see the trees in the Square de la Trinité. She thought: 'Oh well, let him wait another ten minutes.' This thought filled her once more with delight, and as she strolled through the crowd, she could picture him getting impatient, looking at the clock, opening the window, listening at the door, sitting down for a moment or two, getting up again, not daring to smoke (she had forbidden it him on the days they met), and throwing desperate glances at his box of cigarettes.

She walked slowly along, distracted by everything she saw, the faces, the shops; her steps flagged, and so reluctant was she to get there that she made excuses to stop in front of the shop windows.

At the end of the street in front of the church the greenery of the small park was so enticing that she crossed the square, went into the garden, the children's enclosure, and walked twice round the narrow strip of grass past the fresh-faced beribboned nurses in their gaily-coloured sprigged frocks. Then she took a chair, sat down, and, lifting her eyes to the round clock-face like a moon in the tower, watched the hand go round.

At that precise moment it struck the half, and she thrilled, pleased when she heard it chime. Half an hour gained, plus a quarter of an hour to get to the Rue de Miromesnil, and a few more minutes strolling around—an hour! An hour stolen from her rendez-vous! She would be there hardly forty minutes altogether, and it would be over for one more time.

Goodness, how tiresome it was! The unbearable memory of all past rendez-vous stayed with her like a visit to the dentist—one a week on average for the last two years—

and the thought that it was going to happen again in a very short while made her whole body tense. Not that it was so painful as a visit to the dentist, but it was really tedious, so tedious, so complicated, so long-drawn-out, and such a nuisance that anything, *anything*, even an operation, seemed preferable to her. And yet she was on her way there, very gradually, little by little, stopping, sitting down, taking her time, but nevertheless on her way. Oh, she would rather have given this one a miss, but she had stood him up, this poor vicomte, on two occasions last month and she didn't dare do it again so soon. Why should she go there again? Oh why? Well, because she had got into the habit, and she would have no answer for the unfortunate Martelet if he asked the reason why! Why had she ever begun it? Why? She couldn't remember! Had she been in love with him? Possibly! Not very much in love, but just a little, such a long time ago! He was attractive, popular, elegant, gallant, and at the first glance looked exactly like the perfect lover for a *femme du monde*. The courtship had lasted three months—the normal length of time, an honourable struggle, an adequate resistance—then she had consented, with such emotion, such nervousness, such horrible and delightful fear at that first rendez-vous, followed by so many others, in the little bachelor flat in the Rue de Miromesnil. Her feelings? Seduced, conquered, vanquished, what had her feelings been as she crossed the threshold of the door of this nightmarish house for the very first time? Truth to tell, she could not remember! She'd forgotten! One remembered a fact, a date, a thing, but two years later one did not remember a feeling which had fled so swiftly because it was so light. Oh, she had not forgotten the other occasions, the rosary of the rendez-vous, those tiresome Stations of the Cross, so monotonous, one so similar to another, she felt nauseous at the thought of what would very soon come to pass.

Goodness, those cabs you had to hire to get there, they weren't like other cabs, which you used every day. The drivers guessed, of course. She felt it from the very way they looked at you—and the glances those Paris drivers gave you were terrible! When you consider that in court they always recognize criminals even if they have only given them a lift once in the middle of the night from one street or another to some station; that they do business with almost as many travellers as there are hours in the day, and yet they can trust their memory and be certain: 'That's definitely the man I picked up in the Rue des Martyrs, and put down at the Gare de Lyon, at 40 minutes past midnight 10 July last year!'—Is that not enough to make a young woman quake at the risks she runs going to a rendez-vous, entrusting her reputation to the first driver who comes along! For the last two years on journeys to the Rue de Miromesnil, she had used at least a hundred or a hundred and twenty, if you counted one a week. That amounted to as many witnesses who could testify against her in a crisis.

As soon as she was in the cab she pulled out of her pocket the other veil that was thick and black as a mask and drew it over her eyes. That hid her face, it was true, but as to the rest, the dress, the hat, the parasol, couldn't they be seen, or have been seen already? Oh, what torture it was in that Rue de Miromesnil! She thought she could recognize all the passers-by, all the servants, everyone. Scarcely had the cab come to a halt when she jumped out and ran past the concierge who was always standing at the door to his lodging. That man must know everything—her address, her name, her husband's profession, everything—for concierges are the most astute of policemen! For the last two years she wished to buy his silence on one of those days, to give him, throw to him, a hundred-franc note as she passed in front of him. But not once had she dared make that little gesture of throwing a scrumpled note at his feet. She was afraid—of what? She didn't know! That he would call her back if he didn't understand? Afraid of a scandal? Of people crowding round the staircase? Of being arrested perhaps? In order to get to the vicomte's door she only had to climb to the entresol, and yet it seemed to her as high as the Tour Saint-Jacques! She felt trapped the minute she reached the bottom of the stairs, and at the least little noise in front of or behind her she felt she was choking. Impossible to go back, with that concierge, and the street which cut off her retreat; and if somebody was coming down just at that moment she did not dare ring at Martelet's door but went past it as though she were going on somewhere else! She went up and up. She would have gone up forty floors! Then when everything seemed quiet on the stairs she would run back down, in a panic that she would mistake the landing.

He was there, waiting, dressed in a dapper velvet suit with a silk lining, very chic but a bit ridiculous, and for the last two years he had not altered the way he greeted her, not at all, not by the smallest gesture.

As soon as he had shut the door, he would say: 'Allow me to kiss your hands, my dear dear lady.' Then he would follow her into the bedroom, where, with the shutters closed and the lights on, winter or summer, doubtless because it was rather chic, he would kneel down and look up at her in adoration. The first time this gesture had been very charming, very successful. But now she seemed to be watching Monsieur Delaunay in Act Five of a popular play for the hundred and twentieth time. He needed to vary his theatrical effects.

Then afterwards. Ah, afterwards, that was the hardest part! No, this poor fellow certainly did not vary his effects! He was a very nice man, but so run-of-the-mill!

Goodness, how difficult it was getting undressed without one's maidservant! It was perhaps all right once in a while, but it was hateful to do it every week. No, indeed, a man shouldn't demand such a chore from a woman. But if it was hard enough getting undressed, getting dressed again became almost impossible, and so annoying it would make you scream, and you felt so exasperated you wanted to hit the man who was hovering round you clumsily saying: 'Would you like me to help you?' Help her? Oh yes, with what? What could he possibly do? It was enough to see him holding a pin between his fingers to know the answer to that.

Perhaps that was the moment she had begun to dislike him. When he asked: 'Would you like me to help you?' she could have killed him. And then was it possible that a woman would not in the end hate a man who for the last two years had made her get dressed without her maidservant more than one hundred and twenty times?

It was true there weren't many men as gauche as he was, as dim, as boring. That little Baron de Grimbal would not have asked in that foolish fashion 'Would you like me to help you?' He really would have helped, he was so quick, funny, witty. Well, there you are! He was a diplomat; he was someone who had been around a lot, frequented a host of women, and had no doubt helped them out of, and back into, outfits from the world over!

The church clock chimed three quarters. She sat up, looked at the clock-face and murmured, with a laugh: 'Oh, he must be getting really agitated by now!' Then, walking more briskly, she left the little park.

She had not gone ten paces across the square when she came face to face with a gentleman who made a deep bow.

'Oh, is it you, Baron?' she said in surprise. She had just been thinking of him.

'Indeed, Madame!'

And he asked after her health, then after making small talk, went on:

'Do you know that you are the only one—of my women friends, if I may?—who has not yet come to see my collection of Japanese art?'

'But my dear Baron, a woman can't pay a visit to a bachelor just like that!'

'What? What? That's a mistake when it's a question of seeing a rare collection!'

'Well in any case, she cannot go alone.'

'Whyever not? I have entertained crowds of women on their own, just to see my paintings! I receive them every day. Do you want me to tell you their names? No, I shan't tell you. One has to be discreet even in an entirely innocent matter. In principle it's only improper to visit a man who is serious-minded and well-known in a certain situation, if one goes there for a reason that cannot be admitted!'

'Yes, what you say is quite right.'

'So will you come and see my collection?'

'When?'

'Straight away.'

'Impossible. I'm in a hurry.'

'Come now! You've been sitting in the park for half an hour.'

'Were you spying on me?'

'I was watching you.'

'But truly, I am in a hurry.'

'I'm sure you are not. Admit you are not in very much of a hurry.'

Madame Haggan began to laugh, and confessed:

'Well no...not in very much...'

A cab was passing, close to where they stood. The little Baron cried:

'Driver!' and the cab stopped. Then, opening the door:

'In you get, Madame.'

'But Baron, it's impossible, I can't today.'

'Madame, what you are doing is ill-advised. Do get in! People are starting to look at us, you will draw a crowd around you. They'll think I'm kidnapping you and arrest us both. Get in, I beg you!'

She got in, in panic and bewilderment. Then he sat down beside her, saying to the coachman: 'Rue de Provence.'

But suddenly she cried:

'Oh my goodness, I was forgetting a very urgent telegram, could you first take me to the next telegraph office?'

The cab pulled up a little further along in the Rue de Châteaudun, and she said to the Baron:

'Could you get me a fifty-cent card? I promised my husband to invite Martelet to dinner tomorrow, and I completely forgot.'

When the Baron returned holding her blue card, she wrote in pencil:

'My dear friend, I am very poorly. I have terrible neuralgia and must stay in bed. Impossible to go out. Come and have dinner tomorrow evening so that I can be forgiven. Jeanne.'

She licked the envelope, closed it carefully and wrote the address:

'Vicomte de Martelet, 240, Rue de Miromesnil', then, giving the card back to the Baron:

'Now would you be so kind as to put this telegram in the box?'

Tableau Parisien

Octave Mirbeau

It was a week ago, on the Boulevard Saint-Michel, opposite the Lycée Saint-Louis, at about nine o'clock at night. A heavy wagon loaded with blocks of stone was crawling up the hill, dragged painfully by five horses. At that point the incline is rough and difficult. The wagon, like all wagons, was no doubt overloaded, for the beasts, exhausted by their efforts and dripping with sweat, came to a halt. The carter put a wedge under the wheels and let his horses get their breath, for their flanks heaved as they panted and struggled for air.

'Useless bloody creatures!' cried the carter. 'That's at least the tenth time they've stopped.'

He could have whipped them, but he didn't seem to be a cruel man. He placed the whip around his neck and re-lit his pipe, which had gone out.

A little group of idlers had formed round the wagon, and were looking on, at what, they did not rightly know, swapping remarks and recollections which moreover had no relevance to what was going on. They were chatting about the countryside, rampant horses, mad dogs, Sarah Bernhardt, the Exhibition.

When the carter had decided that the horses had rested enough, he tried to get them going again. But their muscles had stiffened up. In vain the poor animals stretched their necks under the whiplash, strained their cruppers, pawed at the ground with their hooves. The cart would not budge.

A woman said:

'It's too heavy! Whatever are they thinking of loading up the wagon like that!'

A man said:

'Huh! It's a bad show if five horses can't pull two wretched blocks of stone.'

Another, wearing a Panama hat, said:

'More building stone! More construction! Can't he see this property boom will end in a crash?'

'That's right,' a third man agreed. 'It's madness.'

More oaths from the carter.

And the group of people got larger. Soon it became a crowd, an agitated, chattering crowd of all the many elements of Parisian society.

Suddenly a very elegant young man, followed by a group of friends, caught hold of the the lead horse by the reins, declaring:

'I know about horses! You'll see. I'll be able to get them going!'

And in a sudden, furious voice, he shouted:

'Giddy up, you old nag!'

He simultaneously raised his cane and belaboured the animal's head with it.

'Get up there, geddup, you filthy old nag!'

The animal stepped back, reared up slightly, in my opinion more offended by the young man's foolishness than by the blows of his cane. The carter let him get on with it, shrugging his shoulders philosophically, his cap tipped right back on to his neck.

'Giddy up, giddy up!'

And the young man hit him with all his strength. A trickle of blood came from a scratch on the nostrils of the animal, which was gently retreating, not trying to defend itself, no doubt, because it was used to being struck.

The crowd admired the young man's boldness, egging him on and echoing:

'Giddy up there, get up!'

At that point a woman accosted the young man:

'Please stop, Monsieur. You have no right to beat horses like that.'

'No right?' he retorted. 'Huh, listen to her! No right to beat horses! She's off her head!'

Bravely, the woman insisted:

'No, Monsieur, you have no right. What you're doing is shameful.'

'You mind your own business! What do you mean—no right?'

And he turned to the onlookers.

'What a slut!' he exclaimed. 'You carry on walking the streets, that's your business!'

There were a few laughs in the crowd, especially since these remarks were punctuated by even more violent blows aimed at the horse.

'Get up there, get up!' shouted the crowd at the horse and the woman, including both in the same scorn and hatred.

The woman did not rise to the insult. She said simply and firmly:

'Right, I'm getting the police.'

The jeers continued.

'Take care they don't send you to Saint-Lazare!'

'Listen to me, Mademoiselle!' And the carter went on swearing:

'For God's sake!'

After a minute or two the woman returned with two policemen. Once the affair was explained, despite the crowd who were clearly on the side of the young man, they found him to be in the wrong. And, after asking his name, occupation and address, with due formality they drew up a case against him.

'I don't believe it!' protested the young man. 'Do you mean to say you don't have any right to beat horses nowadays! That's a fine thing, then! Soon we shan't be able to shoot rabbits! And we are supposed to be free! We are in a Republic! Some Republic!'

He invoked all the high principles of liberty. In vain. After which the police made the dissatisfied crowd disperse, also protesting.

'Yes, he's right! All for a wretched nag! If it was a citizen they wouldn't make such a fuss! They have the right to beat citizens, but not horses!'

The young man, before obeying the instructions of the police, shouted heroically, waving his hat:

'Long live liberty!'

Another showed the horse his fist.

'Get lost then, you supporter of Millerand!'

More oaths from the carter, without it being clear to whom or what they were addressed.

As for the horses, heads down, standing there, manes in a tangle, hocks all bruised, they seemed very humiliated to learn that they were inferior to this collection of foolish and savage people. They said to each other, with that modesty which is typical of them and means that they are unaware of their strength and beauty:

'If men, kings of creation, are so stupid and ugly, what will become of us poor horses?'

The young man, followed by his friends, who had been joined by a few spontaneous admirers, went down the boulevard in triumph. Then he took a seat outside a café. He was very excited and a revolutionary eloquence was boiling away in his soul.

'So,' he cried, 'this is a free country. And I am not allowed to do as I please!... Hit animals, if that's what I want to do... And piss wherever I like... It's monstrous!... Always constraints and limits put on the development of human needs! Well, I for one don't call that liberty. Liberty is running over dogs, beating horses and pissing wherever you like. That's what liberty is.'

'Bravo, bravo, bravo!'

'If I was the king of France, or the Emperor, or the President of the French Republic, I would issue a decree in this form: "Article the first: It is permitted to piss wherever one likes."'

'That's right, wherever one likes!' repeated his friends.

The young man continued:

'And that would be the only article in the decree, for it comprises all the other liberties. That's what I understand by liberty.'

And to enthusiastic acclaim, he ordered some beers.

Rue de la Tacherie

Arnaud Baignot

On finishing my literary studies, and arriving in Paris with small prospect of a career, I was lucky enough to receive a favourable reply to my seventh or eighth application for the post of part-time library assistant.

When my first temporary contract ran out, the librarian, pleased by my discretion, as well as by my serious attitude, proposed renewing it, and moreover suggested the possibility of my taking on some administrative tasks in the mornings, an offer I promptly accepted.

I'd already been working for several months when I left my little flat later than usual on the day of the Coincidence; but this uncharacteristic lateness was symptomatic of a whole string of difficulties I had in getting things off the ground, so I was by now in a bad mood.

Despite the alarmingly advanced hour and the distance separating me from my goal (at that time I lived in a working-class district in the north-east of the capital and I had to get to the heart of the Latin Quarter) I walked to work. I found travelling in the metro depressing. It wasn't the close proximity to others I dreaded so much as the corroboration of my own feelings of mediocrity, weariness and irritation reflected in the faces of that many people so early in the morning. Walking was the only way I could wake up quietly and face the world.

In this race against the clock I was simply the eyes for a pair of legs moving against a backdrop of abstract lines. I viewed the city as a futurist work of art. With my athletic stride I hoped not only that my colleagues would be indifferent as to when I crossed the finishing line, but also that I should have an opportunity before that to enjoy a mouthful or two of strong coffee at the bar of a café where I had acquired this habit.

At the Pont au Change, two thirds of my journey done, I had made up time, so I slowed down as I came to one of the last pedestrian crossings on my route.

Then, out of the corner of my eye, among the numerous feet I encountered, I noticed a pair wearing shoes that were the spitting image of my own. Intrigued, I turned and saw a man roughly my height dressed very smartly and smoking a cigarette; he passed me and disappeared in an unhurried sort of way—towards horizons that were not mine. This stranger, for some unexplained reason, made a strong impression on me. Perhaps because, unlike others who appeared to be bowed down beneath the burden of their lives, there was a lightness in his bearing and he seemed almost to be floating on air.

I arrived on time, by the skin of my teeth. I threw off my coat and nodded briefly at my colleagues; they returned my greeting without speaking.

It was a long day.

Some days later, in the same place and roughly at the same time, I came across the same individual wearing my shoes. On an impulse I decided to follow in his footsteps, which brought us, to my enormous relief, to a bar a few streets away in the Rue de la Tacherie.

The stranger sat down outside the café, lit up a cigarette, and ordered a coffee from the waiter. I spied on him while I drank my *express* at the bar.

The smoke rings he blew formed intricate pathways in space.

He opened a newspaper.

It seemed as if he were going to spend his morning thinking, reading, perhaps writing. He behaved like someone for whom time was of no consequence.

While I was reflecting on these things, I glanced at the clock opposite; there was no possibility I would arrive on time in the library; there was every possibility I would be the last. I hurriedly paid for my drink and, without turning round, tore myself away from this fascinating place.

The next day, thanks to a renewal of energy, I was the first to arrive at work. The colleague who usually won first prize wore a dubious expression. The following day, however, in a few seconds, I laid waste my efforts of the day before. I can't think what impulse made me follow the stranger who crossed my path again.

We found ourselves in the same café as before and more or less in the same spatial relation to one another, and—could it be?—in the same frame of mind.

I spent a considerable time watching the grey snakes that curled out of the burning end of his cigarette. I also studied his gestures while he was writing whatever it was in his obviously well-filled notebook.

I suddenly felt like a smoke too. I went over to his table and asked him brusquely for a cigarette. He nodded to me to help myself from his packet, before holding out the flame of his lighter for me.

The same scenario was played out several mornings in a row (the only difference being that I always had my own cigarettes after that). Before long I no longer bothered to follow him: I waited outside the café with my coffee, my newspaper and my notebook.

My late arrivals at the library got to be a habit. I found the work increasingly unbearable. I carried out my tasks without conviction, without motivation, and without the energy which doubtless characterized my work when I'd been on top form. Nor did I put on a brave face or whisper the words of encouragement to myself that helped me onwards when the going got tough.

One evening I left the library several minutes before the authorized time, without troubling to tell my colleagues. The more time went by, the more marked my lateness became. I was reprimanded; I mumbled silly excuses.

One morning I couldn't tear myself away from the table next to the other man. I even watched him leave. I turned up at the library at the beginning of the afternoon, giving as my excuse that I'd been prevented from coming in earlier by illness. The vibes from my colleagues, as expected, were hostile: meaningful glances lurked along every corridor, behind every door. I, for my part, tackled my administrative tasks morosely and cast the evil eye on my comrades when their backs were turned.

* * *

I didn't see him for several days. I wondered where he was. One morning from outside the café where I had acquired my new habits, I spied him walking rapidly along one of those suffocating boulevards full of hooting cars, whose pavements I had trodden for so many months.

I rose swiftly, paid and ran after him. Despite my best efforts, I lost track of him quite near the place I'd been working at not long before. I hadn't set foot in that district since the abrupt termination of my contract. I never guessed I'd be back so soon.

The clock had not yet struck nine (the time at which my former colleagues normally started work) when, from a discreet observation post, I watched them running like cockroaches towards the entrance to the library, followed closely by the stranger.

Handshakes were exchanged; and I observed a few smiles.

Old Iron

Émile Zola

I was strolling recently along the Quai Saint-Paul, a path honoured until now by the demolition men of the Second Empire. I love these secret places in the capital where the houses still retain their individuality and are not lined up in that dreadful uniform fashion, like army barracks.

On the opposite bank the dark mansions of the Île Saint-Louis are slumbering, as though lost in the shadows and silence of the last century. The greenish river flows beneath, with large murky drifts of ever-changing shot silk. Upstream it widens, blocked by the timbers of the Estacade which protrude like the buttresses of some ancient wooden cathedral. A huge curtain of blue sky rises then, edged green by the trees of the Jardin des Plantes in the distance. You would think yourself a hundred leagues away from the Rue de Rivoli, in some town in Holland with vast shining horizons.

What I find particularly fascinating about the Quai Saint-Paul are the shops, the little low, narrow shops, in their charming simplicity. How far removed we are here from the luxurious shops of the exclusive districts! Here the shop windows have a primitive innocence about them. The things for sale do not wear the least dab of make-up— and what things they are! Old jewellery, old clothes, old books, old furniture, old musical instruments, a museum full of good old Parisian junk.

* * *

As I walked along, face to the wind, I came to the most curious shop, the most astonishing you ever saw. Behind its panes, grey with dust, was ranged a bizarre collection of rusty iron on half-rotten shelves. There were bits of keys, nails, blades of daggers, an unbelievable array of nameless junk. A layer of caked mud made permanent by the rust covered these objects, which must have been in the water for some time.

Following my instinct I went in, and realized I was in one of those curiosity shops whose speciality is selling rare objects pillaged from the Seine. It's a whole industry. In the summer when it's hot and the water is low, the river discloses its treasures. The river-bed apparently contains priceless riches, Roman swords, chassepot barrels. Collectors are very hungry for that sort of thing.

The shop I had just entered was absolutely jam-packed with old metal objects. I did not know where to put my feet. A skinny little old man, ferret-faced, rather dark of complexion, received me brusquely like a professor who had been importuned in his laboratory.

* * *

This little old man was wearing those old-fashioned round spectacles, a pale green, which in an odd way made his eyes look bigger, exactly like a barn-owl. He greeted me in a cracked, quavery voice that sounded like the cackling of the devil.

'Season going well?' I asked.

'Pretty well,' he answered, without appearing surprised at my familiar tone. 'As you see. I am sorting out my recent acquisitions.'

In front of him he had a pile of iron that was still wet. He picked up each fragment with delicate fingers, wiped it lovingly, turned it over and over, and with a little chuckle of delight, placed it on a table.

'The waters are low at the moment,' I went on after a silence. 'They must have discovered some curious things.'

'Oh yes! Some amazing things! This last week I've acquired this heap that you see here. You wouldn't credit what rare pieces there are in that lot.'

The pile looked to me to be horribly dirty. I bent down for a closer look, giving this heap of rust my full attention but not daring to touch it. In my ignorance, I wasn't able to recognize so much as a nail.

The little old man quivered with pleasure.

* * *

Then suddenly he took a piece from the heap and said triumphantly:

'You see this piece? You are wondering what it is?... Young man, it is nothing less than the "device" Monsieur Rouher used to declaim his great speeches to the Legislative Assembly. This little instrument, which he borrowed from one of his puppeteer friends in his lodgings in the Champs-Élysées, was the joy and tranquillity of France for many many years. One day as he was trying it out on the Pont de la Concorde watching the river flow, the clumsy fellow let it drop. And you know how this sad story ended.'

I respectfully admired the 'device' of Monsieur Rouher. As I retreated I stepped on a small piece of metal and nearly broke it in two.

'Watch out!' the shopkeeper shouted in anguish. 'You are ruining the left side-piece of the spectacles worn by Monsieur Ollivier the day when, on the road to Damascus, he saw the imperial eagle in all its glory. Today the road to Damascus leads to the Ministry of Justice. Yes, that's the left piece, on the side of the heart...'

He stopped, and shouted at me. He cast angry looks in my direction; as I withdrew my foot I had had the misfortune to stand on another object.

'Damn you, young man, be careful! Now you are crushing a probe which was used on a noble personage. It is an invaluable piece. It will be displayed one day in the Musée des Souverains.'

The little old man kept quiet for a moment in front of the three objects he had just placed on the table. Then he laughed softly. Behind his spectacles his eyes turned a strange green and I thought I saw his pointed nose twitch with glee.

He muttered in a squeaky voice:

'The "device", the broken pair of spectacles, the noble probe: the whole of the Empire!'

* * *

I didn't dare move. I made myself small, fearing to be thrown out. The old man having calmed down again, I was bold enough to ask him a question.

'What's that strange rosary?' I asked.

'That rosary', he replied with his demonic chuckle, 'is made of the bullets loosed in Paris 2 December 1851. It belonged to the Duc de Morny, who used it night and morning when he was saying his prayers.'

'And what about this—another bullet?'

'No, that's a toy, a marble the Prince Imperial used to play with. Monsieur Clément Duvernois came to buy it off me to set in a brooch to wear on his tie. I am asking 100,000 francs. He's offering 90,000. We shall come to some agreement in the end.'

'Oh, at last here's one thing I recognize! It's a piece of barbed wire, isn't it?'

'That? Oh you poor man! Don't you recognize one of the knitting needles the Empress used when she sat in on the Council of Ministers?'

I apologized humbly, and made the exclamations of astonishment about the Empress's knitting needle that it warranted.

* * *

Meanwhile, the little old man was becoming more animated. Feverishly spreading bits of iron in front of me he named the objects one by one, indicating in a few words the origin and use of each. This man was a catalogue, the most extraordinary catalogue you could ever imagine. From time to time his glaucous, barn-owl eyes glanced palely at me through his green spectacles, and his voice took on the earnest accents of a madman, interrupted by outbursts of bitter sarcasm.

'A letter-opener made of fine steel, a thin blade in use for twenty years in the *Cabinet Noir*. You can see how the blade has worn away after some dreadful infamy or another.

'The buckle of a garter belonging to Princess ***, that queen of elegance who sets the trend for high- and low-born Parisiennes. I admit I haven't been able to discover why it ended up at the base of the second pillar of the Pont Royal opposite the Tuileries. But one couldn't be in the least doubt about its authenticity. It is well known to many gentlemen, who have vouched for it.

'A musical tobacco pouch which the honourable Monsieur Belmonter is said to have lost one night leaving the Chamber, when he went fishing under the Pont des Arts.

'This tobacco pouch plays only one tune—"Reine Hortense". But it's very tinny. A dark lantern, from among the things having to do with the coup d'état. The water couldn't wipe out the bloodstain that reddened the handle. The truncheon belonging to a doughty police sergeant. A fistful of blond hair is still sticking to this weapon of pacification. Some woman, some child of eighteen or twenty, in trouble for going back home after spending fourteen hours in a workshop.

'An iron box which contained the papers concerning the famous conspiracy investigated in vain by Monsieur Piétri. I opened the box. It was empty. The fish had eaten the papers and I don't think fish can talk.

'Prince Pierre's revolver, an article that all Italian bandits will fight over for gold.'

* * *

And the little old man went on and on. His voice grew flute-like, his green spectacles flashed. He bent down to go on naming the objects with ever more enthusiasm, when I stopped him by touching him on the shoulder.

'Enough!' I said. 'I am lost in admiration. I can't keep up with you.'

Then in a sarcastic voice:

'Aren't you going to buy anything?' he enquired.

'Alas, I am only a poor journalist, I wouldn't be able to afford one of these rare curios.'

The little old man had an attack of coughing.

'All right, all right. So I shall make you a present. Choose whatever you like.'

I must have seemed very hesitant.

'Oh, you can't decide,' he went on, with a dry laugh. 'Damn it! I understand...Monsieur Rouher's "device" is very tempting, is it not? But the Duc de Morny's rosary and the musical tobacco pouch of Monsieur Belmonter are not to be sneezed at either...Come now, do you prefer the noble probe or the Prince Imperial's marble, or the sergeant's cosh?...'

I still hesitated. Suddenly he clutched his forehead.

'Oh, I see what you would like. You are eyeing the Empress's knitting needle with a veritable passion. Ah, young man, you are asking rather a lot!'

In vain I protested, swore to Almighty God that I had not had my eye on the Empress's knitting needle; he thrust it into my hands, saying with one last burst of laughter:

'If tomorrow France wants to busy herself with politics, you will tell her to run away and do her knitting instead!'

Rue Saint-Sulpice

Marcel Aymé

Normat was a maker of sacred images. He possessed four metres of window space in the Rue Saint-Sulpice and photographic workshops looking out onto a courtyard at the back. One morning after examining the sales statistics he took down the speaking-tube that connected with Studio H. 'Ask Monsieur Aubinard to come down to the shop straight away.' While waiting for his workshop manager, Monsieur Normat jotted down some numbers on a piece of rough paper.

'Monsieur Aubinard, I have asked you to come here in order to inform you of the latest sales figures. For Christs and Saint John the Baptists they are not good. I will even go as far as to say they are abysmal. In the last six months we sold 47,000 adult Jesuses compared with 68,000 in the same period last year, and the turnover of Saint John the

Baptist went down to 8,500. Take note that this steep decline follows immediately on the improvement of our photographic equipment in which we invested heavily, at your behest.'

Aubinard made a weary gesture which indicated higher preoccupations than those of his employer.

'The crisis,' he murmured bleakly, 'it's definitely the crisis.' Monsieur Normat, crimson in the face, got up from his armchair and went over to Aubinard menacingly.

'No, Monsieur. There is no crisis in the buying and selling of sacred images. It's a hateful lie. How dare you speak of crisis for our specialities when all decent people are lighting candles to the recovery of our economy and doing their best to conciliate Heaven by the presence of our Lord?'

Aubinard apologized and Monsieur Normat, going back to his armchair, continued:

'Monsieur Aubinard, you will judge for yourself how loathsome your defence is when I have proved to you that the shop has not registered the slightest drop in the sales of other objects. Come here, look at the figures... The three-coloured Virgin continues at 15,000... Baby Jesus also sells regularly. Look at Saint Joseph, the Flight into Egypt, little Sister Teresa... I'm not making it up, the numbers speak for themselves. Take Saint Peter and Saint Paul. And you can look wherever you like, even at the more specialized saints. I read: Saint Anthony 2,715 last year, 2,809 this year. Do you see?'

Aubinard, leaning over the file, risked, in a feeble voice:

'They say people are losing interest in Christ…'

'Stuff and nonsense. I happened to speak to Gombette from the Rue Bonaparte the other day. He gave me to understand that Christ has never been so popular.'

Aubinard stood up again and took a few steps towards his boss's desk.

'Of course,' he sighed, 'but Gombette only makes reproductions from the Louvre, he doesn't create them from life…Oh, I know what you'll say: we have perfected our photography processing, the price is excellent, and there is no reason why our Christs should not sell as well as the Holy Virgin or Sister Teresa, since we lavish the same amount of care on all of them. I know…'

Monsieur Normat studied his workshop manager with a worried curiosity.

'A fault in the composition?'

'I've been doing this job for a long time,' objected Aubinard, 'and you saw what I did with the Martyrdom of Saint-Symphorien: there have probably never been two such successes outside of my workshop.'

'Well then?'

'Well…'

Aubinard was showing signs of impatience. He exploded:

'The reason is that you don't see one Christ in the whole of Paris! It's over, I'm telling you, there are none left! Who wears a beard nowadays? Parliamentary deputies or employees in ministries, along with a dozen painters that look like tramps. All right, you try to spot a nice-looking boy in all that mess. Let's suppose that you find one and he takes on the job. You waste a fortnight in the first place waiting for him to grow some hair on his chin and when he has let his beard grow he looks like a bogus monk or a pharmacist in mourning. You can't imagine how many you need to throw away…Listen, only last month I got through six, and in the end not one was usable. Oh, those people who work on the apostles or the female saints don't get frustrated like that. An old man is always an old man and if it's an apostle, the customers don't study him too critically; and there are hundreds of little trollops who'll look like virgins for you…'

Monsieur Normat's face grew sterner. He disliked such crudeness in his staff.

Aubinard sensed the disapproval and went on more calmly:

'A Christ must be young, bearded and good-looking. Are you telling me such people exist? Well, it's not as easy as that. But what is rarer, and what you must have, is a man with a distinguished face and gentle eyes. But he must not look penniless either, you know that as well as I do. The public doesn't like people looking poor. It's not easy, you know. I despair of ever finding someone like that. There are none left in Paris. So you can see what I've been working at lately, the Garden of Gethsemane. It's careful, finished, nothing to criticize on that score, but the model had eyes like a cow, no more tormented than if he were drinking his aperitif. And besides I had to glue on a false beard, he was too young to have one of his own. As a result—my Christ looks like a fellow from the Comédie Française, and don't go telling me I should do it again. If he's not naturally like that…'

'Quite right.'

'And what I am saying about my Christ, I could just as well say about my John the Baptist, apart from his beard.'

Monsieur Normat, deep in thought, left his office and paced up and down his shop, hands behind his back. Aubinard allowed his eyes to wander in a vague and melancholic way to the shop window, dreaming of the ideal face whose image pursued him everywhere, even into his slumbers. Suddenly he had a violent shock: between the portrait of the Pope and the effigy of Little Sister Teresa, *there was Christ*, breathing a fine mist on to the glass. He wore a hard detachable collar and a soft hat, but Aubinard was not mistaken. He hastened to the shop entrance, stepped on to the pavement and found himself face to face with a man, poorly, but decently, clothed. A resigned face with eyes that were both tender and innocent was framed by a fine beard. Aubinard, motionless at the door, stared hungrily at him. The man felt this penetrating stare, bowed his head and took a startled step back. Aubinard sprang forward like a wild animal, seized him by the arm, and turned him round, but the stranger raised such terrified, troubled eyes that the workshop manager was quite overwhelmed.

'I'm so sorry,' he stammered. 'Have I hurt you?'

'Oh, no,' replied the man gently.

And he added, mournfully, but modestly:

'Though plenty of others have looked at me like that.'

'I'm sure,' murmured Aubinard, still troubled.

They contemplated one another in silence. The man did not even seem to be waiting for an explanation, as if he were resigning himself to an adventure whose outcome had been determined since the beginning of time. Aubinard's throat was tight with pity and an inexplicable sense of remorse. He suggested timidly:

'It's cold this morning... Perhaps you are chilly. Would you like to come inside for a moment?'

'Oh, yes, that would be nice.'

As they entered the shop, Monsieur Normat threw a suspicious glance at the stranger and shouted from the back of the shop, 'What's going on?'

Aubinard said nothing. He had heard the question, yet he suddenly felt hostile towards his employer. He fussed around his guest, making solicitous remarks which irritated Monsieur Normat.

'I'm sure you must be tired... Yes, you must be very tired. Come and sit down over here.'

Carefully he conducted him to the office and made him sit down in his employer's armchair. Monsieur Normat brought himself up to his full height, and, marching to his office, repeated in a fierce voice:

'What's going on?'

'No, no, it's all right. Don't you see that it's *Christ*?' Aubinard threw this out indignantly over his shoulder.

Monsieur Normat was taken aback. Then he had a good look at the man who had sat down in his armchair and agreed:

'That's true. His head is right. But all the same that's no reason to...'

Aubinard was standing, happy and smiling, in front of the chair.

Monsieur Normat, annoyed, said roughly:

'And is he willing, your fellow?'

Aubinard had lost sight of his professional preoccupations. The words of his employer brought him back to them. Although it was an effort, he studied his model less disinterestedly. 'His features are a bit strained,' he mused, 'but that's not a bad thing—on the contrary. I think he'll make us a first-class "Ecce Homo". The first few days we'll put him on the Cross, afterwards we'll do a Garden of Gethsemane, and when we've fed him up a bit he can be the Good Shepherd, "Come unto me…"'' In a few seconds he had calculated all the evangelical successes he would be able to extract from this unexpected Christ. The man seemed embarrassed by the twofold examination of which he was the object. His worried look was still having an effect on Aubinard, who felt uneasy about questioning him.

'What were you doing before this?' asked Normat. 'And what's your name, anyway?'

'Machelier, Monsieur,' replied the stranger humbly, as though hoping the first question would be forgotten.

Monsieur Normat repeated the name several times to make sure he was pronouncing it correctly, and, addressing himself to Aubinard:

'Keep an eye on him. With that sort there are always surprises. You don't even know where he's from.'

Machelier jumped up from the chair in sudden anger.

'I'm just out of prison,' he said. 'And I don't owe you anything.'

He made for the door. Aubinard caught him and taking him by the arm put him back into his employer's armchair. Machelier, surprised at his own temerity, did not put up any resistance. His mind on the statistics, Normat was regretting his hastiness.

'Twenty francs a day,' he suggested, 'how would that suit you?'

Machelier appeared not to have heard.

'You want twenty-five? All right, we'll pay you that.'

Slumped in his chair, Machelier said nothing. Aubinard leaned over and whispered:

'The boss is offering you twenty-five francs a day. Usually people only get twenty. Is that agreed? Twenty-five francs. Come up to the workshop with me. The work isn't difficult.'

The two men left the shop and, after crossing a courtyard, entered a dark stairway.

'They gave me a six-months sentence, not suspended,' Machelier said. 'Oh, that wasn't too bad considering what I'd done to them. In prison I saved a bit, but now...'

'You'll get paid before long. Two days in advance if you like.'

They arrived on a landing. Machelier stopped.

'I'm hungry,' he murmured.

He was very pale and out of breath. Aubinard hesitated and almost gave in to an impulse of compassion, but he thought of the possibilities that were offered by this face of a Christ who was hungry, humiliated, imploring. 'When he's eaten, he won't look like that', the workshop manager told himself. 'I must take advantage of it and put him on the Cross without further ado.'

'Be patient for a while, you'll have something to eat at midday. It's ten o'clock already.'

The first sitting seemed to the suffering man to go on for ever. The poses on the Cross were tiring, and in his feeble state they bordered on the painful. He was disgusted at the very sight of the instruments of his martyrdom. Aubinard seemed delighted. He let him go at about one o'clock and, giving him fifty francs as an advance, granted him a rest for the afternoon.

Machelier went in search of a restaurant where he could eat cheaply. When he had devoured two slices of *blanquette de veau* he felt rather pleased with himself. As he cut into his cheese he remembered a time, a few months before he was in prison, when he had led a respectable life as a pianist in a café in Montmartre; he had friends, café-owners were polite when they talked to him. When he greeted the public, girls looked at him adoringly. But unfortunately the violinist had lustrous black wavy hair. With those locks he had seduced a girl that Machelier had designs on himself. Violinists enter women's hearts easily, they prance about on stage, twist and posture and tickle the end of their instruments with clever little movements, and in the long, tapering notes when they close their eyes and stretch their necks, you always want to look at their feet to make sure they are not taking flight. Using his hair to good effect, the violinist had taken the girl to bed, and one day when he was boasting about this, Machelier had slit his throat with a pair of scissors, and come within an inch of killing him.

As he finished his meal, Machelier thought that, after all, the violin-player wasn't dead, since he'd gone back to play in the orchestra. Why should he, Machelier, not be taken on? Being in prison for six months did not mean he did not have great gifts. It seemed to him that he was betraying his calling as an artist if he agreed to strip in a photographer's studio. He persuaded himself, in an optimistic mood due to having eaten, that he would easily find employment, and decided he would go and give the photographer back the twenty-five francs which he had received as an advance. On leaving the restaurant he went and rented a room in a hotel in the Rue de Seine, and, tempted by the soft bed, put off till the next day searching for a job that was worthy of his talents. He fell immediately into a deep sleep which lasted until midnight. He woke up and went back to sleep almost straight away but it was a sleep thronged with nightmares. He dreamed he was crucifying the violin-player, who had a crown of thorns on his head, and that the court condemned him to another six months of prison. He woke with his teeth chattering, scarcely reassured by the daylight. To his bitter remorse of the next morning was added the memory of the torture endured on the Cross. But his resolution had not weakened.

As he went up to Studio H, he was clutching in his pocket the twenty-five francs he proposed to give back to Aubinard.

The workshop manager welcomed him cordially, almost deferentially, and drew him towards a table on which were spread out some photographic prints.

'Look! What work, eh? You must admit that you were astonishing, I'm not exaggerating, astonishing.'

Machelier looked a long time at the prints. He was very moved. When Aubinard asked him to get ready to pose, he undressed without hesitation, with a haste that he himself found surprising. For three days they continued to put him on the Cross; and when the manager judged he had enough crucifixion poses, he made him do some Stations of the Cross. He applied himself to his work with vigour, and Aubinard marvelled at such intelligent zeal. Monsieur Normat soon realized how fortunate he was in this model, for, on sending out prints, he received significant orders for crucified Christs.

Every day the former pianist took home from the studio a dozen photographs of Christ and papered his bedroom walls with them. In the hotel, they thought he was particularly devoted to the Cross. In the evenings when his gaze fell upon these pictures it always gave Machelier a shock. Sitting on his bed he spent a long time recognizing himself in all the Christs. He felt moved by his own suffering face, his torture and his death. Sometimes, when he thought about his judges and his prison, it seemed to him that he had suffered an injustice and it pleased him to pardon his tormentors.

In the studio he never showed signs of impatience, he was gentle, eager to please, and sought any occasion to be obliging to his colleagues. Every one of them appreciated his gentleness and respected his melancholy demeanour. They all agreed he had chosen his job well. He was in fact so well adapted to his character that the people working there were not really surprised by his strange remarks. Aubinard, who was fond of his model, was sometimes disturbed by him and would say to him softly:

'All the same, you mustn't believe it has actually happened to you.'

One morning Saint Peter came in to Studio H to make some enquiry on behalf of the boss of Studio B. He had kept his cardboard halo on his head. When he left, Machelier went to the door with him, saying:

'Go, Peter…' in a grave voice which surprised the good fellow.

In the street Machelier suffered all the time from the indifference of passers-by, not through any human pride but out of pity for them. As he went past churches he said obscure things to beggars and overwhelmed them with promises of glory.

'Just give me a little money,' a beggar outside Saint-Germain-des-Prés said to him.

Machelier pointed to a wealthy-looking man just getting into his car.

'You are richer than him...A hundred, a thousand times richer!'

The beggar called him a shit-heap, and Machelier went away, not in the least resentful but with his head hung on one side and his soul overwhelmed with sadness. One evening in his room he thought about his dead parents and wondered if they were in Heaven. He turned to his picture to commend the two suffering souls, then changed his mind and nodded with a confident smile, as though to say: 'It's pointless, I'll sort it out.'

In the meantime the workshop manager was not far off having exhausted all the reasonable poses with his model, and foresaw that he would soon have to call it a day. In any case Machelier had put on weight and his cheeks were actually rather fat, even for a Christ Triumphant. One morning Aubinard had him posing for a bust with a halo and a large heart in cardboard hanging round his neck when Monsieur Normat came into the studio.

Studying the last negatives he observed to Aubinard:

'They are nowhere near as good as the first ones...'

'That's true.'

'I think you would do well to stop doing Christs. We have a fine collection now, which far outstrips all else done in that style, and I really can't see any point adding to it.'

'I was thinking the same myself. As you see, I haven't done anything worthwhile these last three days.'

'Now what you must do is work on Saint John the Baptist... It's a very popular item and we are deplorably weak in that department, as I've told you already. But we must have something good to give to our travelling salesmen next month...'

'Next month, that's a bit short notice, Monsieur Normat... We should need an exceptional stroke of luck, a meeting like the one with my Christ...'

Aubinard threw a grateful glance at his Christ who was waiting, stroking his cardboard heart, until Monsieur Normat had finished his inspection. Only towards his boss did Machelier abandon his habitual goodwill. He put up with him with an impatience that was full of disgust, and dreamed of getting rid of this florid fat-bellied dealer. Aubinard, who was looking at his model, thinking of the difficulty of finding a Saint John the Baptist, had a sudden inspiration and said to the apprentice:

'Go and get me a razor, a shaving-brush and some shaving cream.'

To Monsieur Normat, who looked surprised, he said, pointing at Machelier:

'He's just at the right stage to be Saint John the Baptist. You'll see.'

The two men drew nearer to the Christ and Aubinard said:

'You're in luck ... We'll cut off your beard and you'll do another week as John the Baptist.'

Machelier looked the boss contemptuously up and down, and, casting reproachful glances at Aubinard, replied:

'I am ready to suffer anything, but I shall not shave my beard off.'

It was no use Aubinard suggesting that his Christ was worn out and that there was no way of keeping him on other than to change him into a John the Baptist. Machelier, who felt that his divinity resided almost wholly in his beard, contented himself with answering:

'I won't let anyone touch one hair of my beard.'

'Come now,' said Aubinard. 'Think it over. You have no money, no job ...'

'I shall never part company with my beard.'

'He's stubborn,' Monsieur Normat said. 'Leave him be. Pay him off straight away and send him packing. What a fool!'

When he had paid another two days' lodging at the hotel, Machelier began to experience pangs of hunger again.

First he was rather proud of it, then, as the hunger began to hurt, he doubted his divine status. One day he remembered he'd been a pianist and made his way to Montmartre. He thought vaguely that he would wander around outside the café where he had suffered injustice for the first time. Machelier pondered that he was nothing but a poor man capable of inspiring pity in those who had known him before.

He set off on foot and, going down to the river banks via the Rue Bonaparte, he saw his reflection in several shop windows. He saw himself carrying the lamb on his shoulders, climbing Calvary, carrying his Cross...He was comforted and moved by that.

'How I suffer,' he whispered, looking at his crucifixion photograph.

Passing the Seine, he found his image again on the Rue de Rivoli, then near the Opéra. Machelier could scarcely feel his hunger any more, was walking slowly, looking in the shop windows, hanging on the hope of a new encounter. He saw himself again near the Church of the Trinity, in the Rue de Clichy. Arriving outside the café where he had played the piano, he passed by very quickly without looking inside. He felt remote from this place in Montmartre, he wanted to go further up. Fatigue and hunger produced a kind of fever in him; he had to halt several times in the course of his ascension. Night was falling when he arrived at the top of the Mont des Martyrs. Outside the basilica the boutique sellers were beginning to put away their religious objects. Machelier had time to see on one display some from the collection he had provided Aubinard with. There was a Good Shepherd, a Christ with the children, a Jesus in the Garden of Gethsemane, the whole of a Stations of the Cross and in a black wood frame an enlarged image of martyrdom. Machelier was dazzled by all this. He went to lean on the stone balustrade and, looking at Paris stretching away at his feet, he was overwhelmed by the certainty of his own ubiquity. The last rays of light in the west ringed the city with a clear narrow ribbon, lights were lit in the distant haze. Trying to make out in all that space the path he had just taken lined with his image, Machelier felt the intoxication of extending over all the city. He felt his presence floating in the evening and listened to the sounds of Paris reaching up to him like a murmur of adoration.

It was almost eight in the evening when he came down from the Butte. He had forgotten that he was weary and hungry, a song of happiness was humming in his ears. In a deserted street he met a policeman and, stretching out his hand, went towards him hesitatingly:

'It's me,' he said with a tender smile.

The policeman shrugged and went off muttering:

'Damned idiot! You'd do better to get yourself home, instead of annoying everybody with your drunken tales.'

Taken aback by this reception, Machelier stood stock-still for a minute, then, shaking his head, he muttered:

'He doesn't understand.'

A sudden worry made him hesitate, he wanted to turn on his heels and go back up to the top of the hill, but his legs would scarcely support him and he was already going down a street towards a gap of light.

On the Boulevard de Clichy, Machelier wandered up and down for a little while amongst the crowd. No one took any notice of him, and the people who did meet his eyes hurried on, afraid he might ask for money. Several times he nearly got run over, and, shivering with fever, he went to sit on a bench. He had only one idea in his head and it tormented him:

'Why don't they recognize me?'

Crossing the boulevard, two girls came close to make fun of him.

'Are you coming, Landru?' an old whore asked him, alluding to his beard.

The two girls began to giggle and the younger one added:

'No, I told you, it's Jesus Christ.'

'Yes, I am,' Machelier agreed.

Freed of his anxiety, he got up to put his hand in blessing upon the two girls. They ran off, jeering:

'Jesus will bring us bad luck, let's go!'

Machelier realized that he must make another effort to persuade people that he was on their side. He decided he would bring the good news to the poor and left the boulevard, to go down into the city. But he didn't see any poor people, he did not meet one single poor person. He cried aloud in astonishment and stopped passers-by from time to time to ask if they had seen any poor people. The passers-by had not seen any. They did not know if there were any.

It was almost midnight when Machelier reached the Pont des Saints-Pères. He felt neither hungry nor tired, nothing but a grim frustration. He remembered that before he had got to know Aubinard, he had slept under that bridge, and he hoped he would find some poor people there. Going down to the river, he found the place deserted. Machelier felt so lonely he wanted to weep; but over on the other bank he saw some men go by who were off to look for somewhere to sleep under the arch. He waved at them and shouted:

'It's me!'

The others stopped, surprised at this call which echoed against the stones.

'It is I! Don't worry, I am coming…'

He walked down the narrow steps which led into the water.

'I am coming!'

One more moment and the tramps on the other bank saw Machelier walking on the water; but when there was no longer anything except a swirl on the surface, they were not sure whether they had just woken up or whether they still had before them the promise of a night's sleep in which they could forget their own wretchedness.

The Freedom of the Streets

Jacques Réda

On foot or on my bicycle, I am no longer under the illusion I can do what I please. Nor do I believe that as I ride or walk I am obeying some pre-ordained plan which will either point me in the right direction or make me lose my way. Rather it seems to me that the streets don't care about who or what I am, but move, dance about of their own accord—and I let myself be moved along secretly sharing in the fun they are having. They vanish, come back, disappear again. In vain I'll try to follow one—then two, then three—to compose some sort of itinerary: other streets always turn up and cut across them, taking me somewhere quite different. But then those too leave me high and dry, and land me in a place where they suddenly don't feel like playing any more. Then I ask myself that old question of characters in stories: 'Where am I?' And that's what I call *having arrived*.

This has only come about, of course, after some time. First the streets had to get used to me, little by little. They had to realize I wasn't looking to set them traps, or use them in some way to my advantage. They had to come round to believing that I was *one of them*, that they shouldn't feel put out by my being there. For I know they get annoyed (stop abruptly, slyly take revenge) if one reduces them to their passive role of simply joining two fixed points, or if one tries to interfere in their history or secret life. So I am content with whatever of them they let me have, through generosity or indifference, in the perpetual movement carrying them along. So they can't complain about my own doings. There is no difference between my way of writing about them and the way they behave. Each sentence, whether it emerges as rectilinear or curving, is still liable to deviate at intersections. Or it bifurcates and the words set off in one direction, when they were trying to say something about another. The simplest sentence leads always to a new crossing point. The most complex of them shatter at a crossroads or finish in a cul-de-sac, having thought they had captured more sense than the words in fact have. One can extract oneself by means of leapings and slidings. Sometimes I've attempted to bring some order into all this, literally with self-imposed plans of work which might allow me to create coherent compositions instead of making these dislocated journeys, in the course of which from one page to the next I don't just change streets, but districts, climates, worlds. I have never succeeded. And perhaps much less through an innate lack of ability than because of the demands of the truth. And the truth is that the freedom of the streets is not susceptible of any sort of good order; we would have to be ignorant or presumptuous to imagine that they can be accommodated into our indexes, graphics, or alphabet, that they allow themselves to be impressed by the names and the numbers we give them. They have their own configuration—and it is fluid since it has to adapt itself to the conflicting needs of their own fate and desire.

Their fate is to dismember space; their desire is to try and re-assemble it, to grasp hold of it or fuse with it. Space fosters a nostalgia for the streets. They feel it above them and all around them. Even as they stifle it, they pursue it, often clumsily, sometimes to the point of exhaustion. Just when they reach it, they hesitate, give up or are taken aback when it reveals itself. Perhaps (like the Rue Stephenson, if we have to cite one street) they are not strong enough to get over a disappointment: that street sets off with a certain enthusiasm towards a horizon of hills, under a large sky. But as it continues, it beholds the vertical wall of the

Rue Ordener in front of it, and above that, what it sees—this street which needs a bit of cheering up, just a tiny amount of imagination—is the picture of uncompromising austerity, the fifty hectares of the goods depot stretching out as far as the Boulevard Ney. At the Porte d'Orléans another street seems to be petrified by the sight of a pusillanimous, chaotic network of gardens, garages, hovels, stadiums, blocks, towers, gaps without any regard to the amount of space stunned there by a sky always hanging over it more or less loose like an old curtain. Drawn elsewhere, tacking this way and that, they besiege space and gently infiltrate it, try also to seduce it by advancing, camouflaged under flowers and trees. The space in question allows itself to be cajoled. Sometimes they even catch it, take it prisoner, bring it back in triumph to the heart of the city, where it will enjoy a luxurious incarceration. You have to admire how it blossoms forth, proves itself, dreams and like a sovereign in exile reigns in the *allées* of the Luxembourg, along the banks by the Louvre, along the esplanade at the Invalides where rather than even doing honour to it, the streets—Saint-Dominique, de l'Université, de Grenelle—seem to be effacing themselves like timid servants in the presence of its glory. But this treatment does not make you forget the sites, all too quickly developed, in which space wearies and languishes, as if it had not the slightest contact with the streets which, nominally satisfied with holding it in deference and respect, themselves, from their rigid perspectives and bricked-up windows, view it without pleasure.

The same is true of all such old, shrewish streets, so full of vice and desperate to force space into their vilest corners, without really knowing if what is torturing them is a rush of affection or the need to murder. But the thinnest crack in the sky between two roofs is enough to let it escape. You can hear them grumbling and its laughter melts into the sky above. Perhaps it's only a game, albeit one without respite, of a rare violence, and in which one ought to permit oneself to interfere as little as possible.

A Rapist Shouts One Night in Montparnasse

Frédéric H. Fajardie

She was just preparing to cross the boulevard, opposite *La Closerie des Lilas* near the Port-Royal metro.

You were in the back of an old metal-grey Simca 1100. You were with three other guys.

She was laughing.

You guessed she must be about thirty-five. She was a real looker, you thought. She was tall, one metre seventy or seventy-five. She was leaving an Indian restaurant on the Boulevard du Montparnasse. Spicy food, glasses of white Sancerre—the manager had said: 'White or red, up to you. It doesn't matter.' He spoke in bad French, and she'd replied in her fluent English. Touched, he had offered them aperitifs the colour of indigo.

She was not at all used to drinking wine. A little tipsy, she snuggled up to her companion, who was singing *Love me tender* softly to her.

You had a really good look at that girl, you hadn't managed to score yourself, so you were even more jealous. You took in her model figure, her extremely slender waist, her long legs, her high heels in the black shoes with laces twined round her ankles. He'd stroked her thigh during the meal, like all lovers driven by lust. Because of that, her black slit skirt had lost a button and the one next to it was undone so that you saw a flash of the tops of her thighs as she pivoted gracefully round to look at her lover, and, clinging to him, give him a passionate kiss. You also saw, from the back of your old banger, how her hair hung over her face in the style of Louise Brooks.

Enraged, you could see she was as beautiful sideways on as from the front, thereby demonstrating you were a good observer of women.

You let down the window and shouted 'Tart!' in a voice almost choking with fury.

She didn't even hear you.

But I realized what was going on, and the words of Ernst Jünger immediately came to mind: 'The hatred of beauty in abject hearts goes very deep.'

* * *

I have come across creeps like you before. Especially when I was in the army.

As soon as they let us out of our horrible barracks on an immense base deep in the countryside we made for Strasbourg. We wore the navy-blue aviators' uniform, with a cap we called a 'cops' hat', instead of the traditional beret the other services have.

Some of us were very proud of this. A technical unit, not many of us, that was surely a good enough reason to view yourself as being somewhat different?

As for me—if you're at all interested—I couldn't have given a shit. In my opinion the army was disgusting whatever service it was and I haven't changed my opinion about that.

As soldiers we were supposed to have some esprit de corps, and while not being *salauds*, not even in the Sartrean sense, we conformed for the most part to what the officers expected of us. Should I make clear to you that this esprit de corps made me want to throw up? Let me tell you I always managed to be in the latrines when the colours were raised, which, as you know, require the military to stand to attention.

So now we understand each other more and more, you *salaud*: there I was sitting in the latrines humming the 'Internationale' to myself, and you on parade, with tears in your eyes, fingers flat on the seams of your trousers, while the

'Verdun tricolore' was being raised, and let's not forget June 1940, Dien Bien Phu and torture in Algeria.

So, I escaped from the band of blue-uniformed soldiers to get away on my own and visit the town, observe the architecture, the buildings... By which time ten or fifteen of you managed to completely surround a woman on her own, a 'tart', and put her off men for ever: it's often the case that creeps like you are having fun as you go and ruin your lives.

* * *

So you let down your window, your rapist face was twisted with scorn, and you shouted out 'Tart!'

Then I raised my arm and put up my little finger. That's an international sign, so successful that you got the message and your pale face disappeared from the window.

Why the hell didn't you come back then with your three little friends?

Did you think, when you saw my formal suit, that I was a cop? A heavily armed gangster? But you acted with common sense. I'm sure that if the four of you had come back, you would have got the upper hand. But I am also sure I would have smashed your head in.

That's what life and—and the opposite of life—is like: it's *you* I'm talking about.

* * *

Can you imagine that, after fifteen years of living together, a man and woman should be more and more in love? To the extent that they hide away to be on their own?

You shouted at the girl I love, but, you see, I had not just picked her up in a night club. In any case, we never set foot in those places. I wasn't just chancing my luck, and she wasn't fair game, though I'm quite sure you must view every woman like that.

I had received a small cheque that I wasn't expecting and I had used it to treat the woman I love. I had my arm round her shoulders, she was holding me round my waist. Less than a minute before the incident, we were passing 164 Boulevard du Montparnasse and I'd said:

'I came past here 7 May 1968, after the big demo. They were just building this block back then. We fought with the cops till two in the morning. Twenty years have gone by so quickly.'

She flashed me a reproachful look.

'You know very well my dad wouldn't let me go on demos at night.'

I was at fault. So, to beg forgiveness, I'd sung very softly:

> *Love me tender*
> *Love me sweet*
> *Never let me go*
> *You have made*
> *My life complete*
> *And I love you so!*

She twirled round and kissed me at the precise moment the car you were in drew level with us.

In our kiss, you git, there was our love, time flying, the regret for some things we hadn't lived together, I mean: side by side. There was desire, tenderness, violence, gentleness and passion. And, I guess, a host of other things which I hope will always be a secret.

A real love kiss, just as you let down the window.

So you didn't feel my fist in your ugly face, and of course I am a bit sorry about that.

Oh well…

You'll croak one day just the same. Of course, all of us will, but you will die without ever having been loved. You will never know the abandonment of love, or what it brings, or that exchange of looks which lasts for the time it takes to breathe when you are making love to someone you love. A look which makes it possible to imagine the idea of eternity…

You will always be unaware of the sweetness of some feelings which are as fragile as Meissen porcelain and as solid as tungsten.

And because you will not know about that, you won't know anything of the beauty of revolt, the pride in rebelling against an unjust social order. You will never feel that solidarity, that camaraderie of those who fight for the same ideas.

I would almost pity you if you weren't a potential Nazi, a little shit of a fascist like all fascists. And even though you were to tell me you voted for Mitterrand or carried the CFDT card, I should still say, and even more so, that you are a fascist.

There are only two camps. You are decidedly in the shitty one.

Good riddance, you jerk, and stew in your misery, since that's your fate.

Listen, I owe you this at least: you have raised the bar and made me see what we're up against. When you vanished I took a good look at the house fronts along the boulevard and said to myself: socialism will triumph when the stones turn to dust.

January–May 1987

Du Mouron, du Sençon pour les
petits Oiseaux.

Lost Street Cries

Julien Green

Amongst all the 'cries' you don't hear any more, who can remember 'chickweed for the little birds'? What disenchanted soul invented this refrain that has such a touching, tender lilt? So soft a little tune you'd think it had quite given up hope of anyone hearing it at all; it was like the faint keening of a secret nostalgia. You used to hear it in certain streets in Paris, the little monotonal musical phrase audible even in the din of the market; it mingled neither in the farmers' shouting nor in the noise of the lorries, it by-passed all that hubbub, just as a woman who was a stranger there might circumvent a crowd of people.

And the person who chanted this mysterious little jingle always walked along as though in a world of her own, even when others were pushing and shoving around her. She maintained an expression of ethereal indifference on her face. In her hand she held an unwieldy bunch of the yellow flowers which she thrust absent-mindedly towards you, as a Ceres in exile might do, offering the symbol of a forgotten religion with no hope of being understood. On her arm a wide, deep basket held her useless merchandise— for why feed creatures that do nothing but sing? Sometimes when her shawl slipped from her shoulders, she would pull it back around her, and her far-away voice was as faint as those of madwomen or sleepwalkers with their incomprehensible nocturnal, sleepy babbling. So it was only little old ladies in their outdated skirts who approached her and drew out of their bags a metal coin with careful and exaggerated gestures. The chickweed would be proffered to them with exquisite grace and they would grasp it in their bony fingers. You almost felt that you had lit on a religious rite when you saw the woman in the slipping shawl place a stalk of chickweed into their heavily veined hands, and the coin given in exchange suddenly took on an aspect of great antiquity and a propitiatory significance.

Rue de la Chine

Joris-Karl Huysmans

For those who detest the rowdy jollity kept bottled up all week and let loose on Paris of a Sunday, or who want to escape the tiresome opulence of the well-heeled districts, Ménilmontant will always be a Canaan, a promised land where one may enjoy the more melancholy pleasures.

Tucked away in a corner of this district is the most extraordinary, most charming Rue de la Chine. Even though it has been truncated and mutilated by the building of a hospital, which adds to its unassuming little houses behind their fences and hedges the grievous spectacle overhead of suffering humanity wandering around in yards bare of trees or flowers, the street has nonetheless preserved the appealing aspect of a country lane enlivened here and there by small gardens and outhouses.

Surviving as it has, this street has been a denial, the very opposite of the big new thoroughfares with their tedious symmetry, and banal straight lines. Everything in it is odd. On both sides of the unpaved road, which has a drainage channel cut down the middle, there is neither rubble, brick nor stone, but boat-timbers, marbled green by moss and stained a golden-brown by pitch, that serve to extend a toppling fence, dragging down a whole bunch of ivy, and threatening to take with it the door which obviously came from a demolition site and is ornamented with mouldings whose light grey paint still shows through from beneath the tan layer formed by the contact of a succession of dirty hands.

That little one-storey cottage can hardly be seen through the spirals of Virginia Creeper in a tangle of valerian, hollyhocks and great sunflowers whose golden heads, losing their petals, show bald patches of black like the rings of a target.

Almost always behind the wooden fence there is a zinc water tank, two pear trees tied together with a washing line, and a vegetable patch with bright yellow marrow flowers, little plots of sorrel and cabbages criss-crossed by the lacy shadows of Chinese lacquer trees and poplars.

And so the road continues, you can only just glimpse bits of red and purple roofs through the breaks in the greenery. As you go on, it gets narrower, and seems to exert itself, twisting, climbing past occasional old oil lamp-posts planted along the way, until it reaches the distressing, interminable Rue de Ménilmontant.

In this vast district, where low wages condemn the women and children to never-ending deprivation, the Rue de la Chine and the ones that join and cross it—like the Rue des Partants and the astonishing Rue d'Orfila, with its odd, circuitous, abrupt detours, its rough-cut wooden fences, its abandoned summer houses, its deserted gardens now completely reverted to nature, full of scrub and weeds— impart a very special peace and quiet.

It's unlike the Plaine des Gobelins, where the poverty of the natural environment is related to the appalling indigence of those who live there. It's more like a lane in the open country where most walkers seem well fed and watered, the place artists choose to go to in search of solitude. It's the haven craved by grieving souls who ask nothing more than a congenial place to rest far away from the crowds. It's for those who have been disinherited by fate, for those crushed by life, a consolation, a relief engendered by the unavoidable sight of the Tenon Hospital, whose high ventilation shafts pierce the skyline, and whose walkways are filled with pale-faced figures bowed down over the lower world which they contemplate with the deep, eager look of convalescents.

This street comforts the afflicted and consoles the embittered, for at the thought that there are poor people lying in this enormous hospital in great rooms full of white beds, your own sufferings and complaints begin to seem childish and empty. And in front of these cottages tucked away in this little street you begin to dream of a delightful refuge, a cosy little hideaway where you could get on with things just when you felt like it and not be forced to hurry the making of a work of art.

It's true that once you have gone back into the city you tell yourself perhaps quite rightly that you would be bored to death cut off from society like that in a little house, in that silent, isolated road. And yet, every time you come and immerse yourself again in the soothing melancholy of this spot, you get the same feeling. It's as though the forgetfulness and peace you might seek in the contemplation of faraway endless shores—you might find them here, all together at the end of a bus route, here in this lost-village lane in Paris while the joyful, distressing tumult of the large poverty-stricken streets goes on all around you.

The Affair on the Boulevard Beaumarchais

Georges Simenon

At ten to eight, when Martin from Betting and Gaming left his office, he was surprised to see the corridor still packed with journalists and photographers. It was very cold and some of them, with their coat-collars turned up, were eating sandwiches.

'Hasn't Maigret finished yet?' he enquired as he went past.

Right at the end of a vast corridor, instead of taking the stairs, Martin pushed open a glass door. As in all the offices of the Criminal Investigation Department, they had not been generous with the lighting. In the middle of that room, next to the Commissaire's office, was a huge circular sofa upholstered in red velvet. A man in hat and overcoat was sitting on it. A few steps away two inspectors stood smoking while the old janitor was having his dinner in a sort of glass cage.

Martin filled his pipe. In a quarter of an hour he would be home having dinner with his family. He'd come over to have a look at what was going on here simply out of interest, because for the last two days everyone had been talking about it.

'All okay?' he muttered to one of the inspectors.

The latter sighed and pointed to the second door, the door to Maigret's office.

'Who's he with?'

'Still the sister-in-law.'

The man, who heard them whispering, raised his head and threw his companions a mournful glance that had a hint of reproach in it. He was a thin, unhealthy-looking individual of about forty—possibly a bit less—with very bleary eyes and a small brown moustache.

'He's been there since this morning,' the inspector whispered again to Martin.

At that instant Maigret's door opened. The Commissaire appeared and, as he didn't close it again, Martin caught sight of a smoke-filled office and the profile of a young blonde woman sitting in a green armchair.

'Lucas!' called Maigret, looking vaguely at the inspectors like a man who can't see very well. 'Run and fetch some sandwiches...Go to the café and get some beers brought up.'

Martin took advantage of this to shake hands with his colleague.

'How's it going?'

Maigret was rather flushed, and his eyes were bright. He looked like a man who would have given a lot for a breath of air.

'Listen,' he muttered, lowering his voice. 'I'll tell you something...If I haven't done with this enquiry by tonight, I'm giving it up...You wouldn't understand that, would you? I can't be doing with it any longer.'

The man on the sofa, who couldn't catch what he was saying, waited in fear and trembling, but the Commissaire went back into his office and the door closed again. Martin finally left; the hand of the clock moved forward one minute and the raised voices of the journalists could be heard.

* * *

Yet this was an affair which had seemed at first completely banal. The previous Sunday in a block of flats on the Boulevard Beaumarchais where there was a pipemaker living on the ground floor, Louise Voivin died suddenly up on the fourth, showing every sign of having been poisoned.

In the homely, rather bourgeois flat, which could have been a cheerful place, there lived, apart from Louise Voivin, her husband, Ferdinand Voivin, a jewellery broker, and her sister, Nicole, aged eighteen.

It was this Nicole that Maigret had had in his office for several hours and who was still holding her own; she was certainly ill at ease and chewing her handkerchief, but, despite the stifling atmosphere, she had all her wits about her.

There was a lamp on the desk, its gigantic green shade dimming the light. Maigret's face, above the lampshade, remained in shadow. But the girl, sitting in a low armchair, was full in the light. The curtains at the window hadn't been drawn, and you could see the raindrops rolling down the black glass panes, sparkling in the reflection of the lights along the banks of the river.

'Someone's gone to get us a drink,' said Maigret, sighing with relief.

He was so hot he longed to take off his collar and waistcoat, whereas his companion was still wearing her grey fur coat, with a hat of the same colour fur which, added to the fact that she had very blonde hair, gave her a Nordic look.

What could he ask her that he had not already asked? And yet he could not quite let her go. He felt vaguely that he should keep her there under observation, while her brother-in-law still waited in the room next door.

Putting up something of a front, he leafed through his file as though he might have a sudden inspiration if he kept on reading the same details over and over.

Despite its apparent simplicity, the first report on Sunday's events, that of the local police, had already something about it that worried him.

> *...On the fourth floor, in a room situated at the back of the apartment, the body of Louise Voivin was found lying on the floor. Doctor Blind, who had been summoned by the family half an hour before, told us she had died a few minutes earlier in terrible convulsions and he attributes the death clearly to a poisoning, criminal or accidental, no doubt brought about by a strong dose of digitalin...*

Then, a bit further down:

> *... We questioned her husband, Ferdinand Voivin, thirty-seven, who claims he knows nothing about it... He declares, however, that for several months his wife had been manifesting signs of depression...*
>
> *... We questioned Louise Voivin's sister, Nicole Lamure, eighteen, born in Orléans, who gave us the same account as her brother-in-law...*
>
> *... We questioned the concierge who declared that Louise Voivin, in a poor state of health, had lived for a long time in fear of being poisoned...*

As it happened it was All Saints' Day, a Sunday. It was raining, a cold rain, and the air smelled of chrysanthemums and church incense when the men from the Public Prosecutor's Office, wet, with muddy feet, made their way towards evening down the Boulevard Beaumarchais to the pipe-maker's shop, which was closed.

But this was an everyday sort of drama, with the atmosphere of almost all criminal investigations. The real tragedy was not yet suspected by the waiting journalists, for it was just now in the overheated atmosphere of his office that Maigret had discovered it.

And he was impatiently waiting for the refreshing taste of a beer, up until then avoiding looking at the girl with the drawn face who was intently studying the corner of his desk.

'Come in!' he cried.

The waiter from the *Brasserie Dauphine* brought the beer and sandwiches, glancing at Maigret's client.

'Is that all right like that?'

'Yes…Take some to the gentleman in the room next door!'

But Voivin, when they tried to give him something to eat and drink, shook his head as if he had entirely lost heart.

* * *

Maigret, still standing, was munching large mouthfuls of sandwich, while his companion was nibbling at hers.

'How long had they been married?'

'Eight years…'

A banal tale of insignificant folk. Ferdinand Voivin, a small-time broker in precious stones, had made the acquaintance of Louise Lamure, whose parents had a shoe-shop, in the course of a stay in Orléans during which he been responsible for valuations.

'So, in other words, you were still just a little girl?'

'I was ten…'

'I suppose', he attempted a joke, 'you weren't in love with your brother-in-law at that time?'

'I don't know…'

He threw her a surreptitious glance and did not feel inclined to laugh.

'So, a year ago, when your father died, your sister and her husband took you in…'

'Yes, that's correct, I came to live with them.'

'And since when, precisely, have you been sleeping with Voivin?'

'Since 17 May.'

She said it clearly, almost proudly.

'Do you love him?'

'Yes.'

Seeing such a frail and passionate woman, you might have imagined Voivin must be a handsome, romantic fellow to inspire such feelings. That was one of the worrying aspects of this tale—the broker was so nondescript that you had to make an effort to remember what he looked like. His very profession was unpoetic. For hours at a time he haunted the cafés of the Rue Lafayette, home of the Jewellery Exchange, and only a month ago he had bought a modest second-hand car. He was, moreover, in poor health.

'And what about your sister?'

'My sister was jealous.'

'Did she love him?'

'I don't know…'

'What did she say when she found the pair of you?'

'She didn't say anything…She wrote to me…Since then, we haven't spoken.'

'When was that?'

'2 June…It was the third time it had happened…'

'In the Boulevard Beaumarchais?'

'Yes…In my bedroom…Ferdinand thought Louise had gone out but she was in the kitchen with the cleaning woman…'

'You never wanted to go and live somewhere else?'

'I did…It was my sister who made me stay…'

'Why?'

'So as to be able to keep an eye on us…She claimed that if I left the apartment it would be too easy for her husband to meet me in secret…'

'And in the apartment?'

'She never left us on our own...She always wore soft slippers, so that she came in silently...'

'How did you manage to live together for months like that without speaking?'

'We exchanged notes...For instance my sister would write: "Put your dirty clothes out for tomorrow..." Or: "Don't use the bath, there's a leak..."'

'What about Voivin?'

'He was most unhappy...From the very start he refused to sleep in his wife's bedroom and he installed a sofa in the living-room...He swore to me that their relationship had broken down completely...'

Maigret counted on his fingers:

'June...July...August...September...October...Five months!...So did you live like that for five months?'

She simply nodded, as though it was self-evident.

'Did Ferdinand never mention getting rid of his wife?'

'Never! I swear to you...'

'And he never asked you to go away with him?'

'You don't know what he's like,' she sighed and shook her head. 'He's very respectable, you see? He's the same when he does business...When he signs a contract, he honours it, come what may...You ask the people he works with...'

'Nevertheless for several months your sister seemed to be foretelling her own death...She wrote three letters to a school friend and in all three talked about being poisoned.'

'I know! My sister had gone a bit crazy. Through all that spying on us… Almost every night she would open my bedroom door, without making any noise, and in the darkness I would feel her hand touch my face to see if I was in my bed and alone…'

'One question. After 2 June you didn't see Voivin any more on your own?'

'Three or four times, away from the apartment… But my sister knew… Each time she was waiting for us at the hotel door… She used to follow me everywhere… Once she went into town in her slippers because she hadn't had time to put shoes on.'

Maigret had been to the apartment which was as nondescript as Voivin himself. He tried to imagine the life of those three… And he came round to asking himself the same questions again, like horses on a carousel going round and round, never finding a way out.

'Did you know that there was a packet of bicarbonate of soda in the bathroom medicine cabinet?'

Everything turned on that. After Louise Voivin's death they had gone through the apartment. They had almost immediately found a glass that had contained medicine. Analysis had shown that it was digitalin in a little water.

But next to the glass was a packet with a label: 'Bicarbonate of soda'. And that packet contained digitalin enough to kill a hundred people.

'What were you doing last Sunday afternoon?'

'What I did every Sunday. It was the worst day of the week. Ferdinand was in the sitting room looking over his bills. I was reading in my room. My sister was probably in hers…'

'What did you have for lunch?'

'I remember that very well…A hare, that one of Ferdinand's clients sent him…'

And she continued to say his name with passion, as though he were the most handsome and extraordinary of men.

'Did your sister's death upset you?'

'No!'

She did not hide it. She even raised her head so that he could see her face.

'My sister made him suffer too much.'

'And what about him?'

'Was he to blame?…He never loved her, I know that… He lived with her for eight years, but he was never happy… My sister was always miserable and in poor health…After the first year of her marriage she had to have an operation and she was never really a proper woman after that…'

* * *

Maigret went out again for a few moments, and, standing in the doorway, looked at the man collapsed on the sofa. He had already questioned him once, the day before, but only briefly, and he hesitated to start one of those interminable interrogations, that for both parties are equally stressful.

'Did he not want anything to eat?' he muttered to one of the two inspectors.

'No…He claims he's not hungry…'

'I doubt that…'

And Maigret, trying to summon up his courage, went back into his office, where Nicole had not moved.

'By the way, since we were talking about illness…Who in the house suffered from stomach problems?'

'Ferdinand,' she replied without hesitation. 'Only occasionally, but he had it sometimes, especially after his palpitations.'

'Did he have palpitations?'

'Well, two years ago, I think it was, he had treatment for heart trouble, but it was more or less cured…'

'You don't know whether your brother-in-law had pains in his stomach these last weeks?'

'Yes, he did!' she said, also very definitely.

'What day was that?'

'The day we were all feeling sick.'

'You don't remember what you ate?'

'I can't remember.'

'Did you call a doctor?'

'No, Ferdinand didn't want to…In the night we all had headaches, nausea, and Ferdinand thought it might be a gas leak…'

'Was that the only time?'

'Yes…At least, the only time it was that bad…'

'Does that mean there were other bouts of illness?'

'I know what you are getting at, Commissaire…But you won't rattle me…Whatever you say I am sticking to my story, because I know Ferdinand is innocent…If somebody poisoned my sister, it wouldn't have been him, it would have been me, and as you can see I'm not afraid to say so.'

'But you didn't?' he asked in an odd voice.

'No…I never dreamed of it…I would have killed her, but not like that, I don't know how…Recently we'd all been ill, it's true…But I'd like to see you in those circumstances… Can you imagine the life we were leading?…At mealtimes there was always one of us who couldn't eat…Do you know how many cleaning women we had in five months?…Eight! As they said, they didn't want to stay in a madhouse…'

She wept, her nerves giving way. This wasn't the first time since the beginning of the interrogation, but she quickly regained her composure and looked Maigret in the eyes as if to anticipate his questions.

'I don't even know if we still opened the windows…And as for me, I had got to the point of not daring to go to the end of the street, knowing my sister would be hard on my heels...'

'So, according to you, your sister committed suicide?'

She said nothing at first, and it was evident that the question worried her.

'In other words you claim your sister managed to get hold of a considerable amount of digitalin and instead of trying to poison you, killed herself?'

'I don't know,' she admitted.

And it was obvious that she didn't believe that either, that it didn't accord with her sister's character.

'So what happened then?'

'It's a mystery...In any case Ferdinand didn't kill her...'

'And what about you?'

But if he hoped to make her crack, he was disappointed. She lifted her head again, and met his gaze, with a touch of irony.

'I think we'd do better to get your brother-in-law in,' grumbled Maigret. 'Or rather...Wait a moment...Would you wait in the next room while I see him...'

'What do you want to say to him?'

Now on her feet, she was losing patience. She was tearing off little bits of handkerchief with her teeth.

'Show him in!' shouted Maigret, opening the door a little. 'As for the young lady, she can wait.'

And he ushered her out in front, showed Voivin the armchair she had just vacated.

'A glass of beer?'

Voivin only shook his head in reply.

'Not hungry?...I'm sorry I kept you waiting...Your sister-in-law had so much to tell...By the way, what are your plans now?'

Making an effort, the broker raised his head, looked in astonishment at the Commissaire, then with mistrust, as though it was only too clear that he wouldn't be allowed to leave.

'One question, Voivin...As Nicole couldn't speak to you when she wanted, because of your wife, I suppose she wrote to you?'

He tried to understand the connection, then shook his head.

'No...'

'Why not? She's very much in love with you, and you with her...'

'It was impossible...My wife would have found the letters. She spent her time going through the apartment, my clothes, even my shoes...'

Maigret sighed. He would have given a lot to see Nicole's passion addressed to someone else, anybody, but not to this mediocre individual, mediocre in everything, even in his despair.

'Could you not have found a hiding-place?'

'I tell you Louise would have found…'

But the Commissaire seemed not to be thinking about that any more.

'Never mind…By the way, I wanted to ask you about something else…When you had heart trouble…'

Ferdinand smiled sadly.

'I was waiting for you to ask that.'

'Well, answer me!'

'Well, yes, I was prescribed digitalin…But I haven't taken it for over two years…'

'Nevertheless you are aware of the effects and they must have told you that in a massive dose…'

'Believe me, Commissaire, I didn't kill my wife…'

'I am convinced that Nicole didn't poison her either…'

'Did you suspect her?'

'No, rest assured! You are telling me you didn't kill your wife. Nicole didn't kill her. And now I'm asking you something which you don't have to answer. Listen carefully, Voivin…Knowing your wife as you do, jealous as she was, capable of putting up with her sister in her house rather than give her a way of meeting you in secret, knowing your wife, I repeat, would you dare to maintain that she might simply have seen an opportunity to kill herself and at the same time leave you both free?…Have a think…'

'I don't know...'

'Come on now! Answer me or don't answer me, but no lies, Voivin...No evasions...'

The man's lips were trembling. And suddenly a foul smell in the room betrayed the physical effect of his panic.

Maigret went and opened the window without a word, came back to his desk and drained the remains of his beer.

'If you like, I'll help you,' he offered gently.

* * *

'I suppose you would prefer me not to get your sister-in-law in?'

Voivin was crying, perhaps from humiliation as much as grief, and Maigret walked up and down while speaking, and did not look at him.

'If I am wrong, stop me...But I don't think I am...Do you go to Antwerp occasionally?'

'Yes.'

'I thought so...To Antwerp and Amsterdam, where the main diamond markets are...There, you were able to get hold of a certain amount of digitalin more easily and with fewer risks than in France, which would explain why our research in Paris and the suburbs was useless...'

'I'm thirsty,' Voivin muttered, his throat tight.

And he was so humble that Maigret was embarrassed. He took a bottle of liqueur from his cupboard and poured out a generous glass for the broker.

'You are not naturally a jolly person…You marry a girl and from the first year of marriage an operation makes her seem several years older from one day to the next…You carry on working, unhappily, but conscientiously as in everything you do, and there comes a time when your heart begins to give you trouble. Is that correct?'

'It wasn't serious…'

'No matter…Now your sister-in-law comes along and suddenly you discover youth and joie-de-vivre…You fall in love!…Madly in love!…But you have too much regard for your vows to abandon your wife and make a new life for yourself…You are weak, cowardly, I might even say. The day your wife found you together, you do nothing…'

'I'd like to know what you would have done in my place!'

'That doesn't matter…Life in the Boulevard Beaumarchais is becoming torture for you every minute of every day…If you are incapable of leaving your wife, you are even more incapable of giving up your sister-in-law…Stop me if…'

'It's the truth!'

'You are the kind of weak character who provokes catastrophes. What I really mean is, you are the sort who, afraid of being left on your own, are capable of dragging others to their deaths along with yourself…Since life was no longer possible, you thought you would all three die, which explains why you bought such a large amount of poison…Is that right?'

'How did you guess that?'

'Up to this point, it was easy... It's your wife's death and only hers I couldn't explain... But you have given me the reason... I'll come to that... First of all, admit that at least twice you held what we might call dress rehearsals. I mean that you put small doses of digitalin in the food, which made you all ill...'

'I wanted to find out...'

'That's right... You were afraid... You couldn't make up your mind to die... And you were trying to work it out with very small doses... As for the rest, your answer to one of my last questions gave me the explanation... Your wife was watching your actions and your movements, going through every nook and cranny in the flat, even your shoes... Where could you possibly put the digitalin in these circumstances?... And what was the medication only you were taking?'

His face drawn, Voivin raised his eyes in silence.

'From then on, everything hangs together. The digitalin is concealed by the innocent label "Bicarbonate of soda"... And you would no doubt have dithered around for weeks, perhaps months...'

'I don't think I could ever have done it!' the broker groaned.

'No matter... You would have hesitated for a long time, anyway, if the accident had not happened... One of your clients gave you a hare as a present...Your wife, in poor health, has trouble digesting it, goes to the medicine cabinet, sees the bicarbonate of soda and puts a spoonful in her glass...'

Voivin hid his face in his hands.

'That's all.' Maigret brought the conversation to a close and opened the window a bit more...'Tell me...There's a washroom next door...Do you want to use it before I call your sister-in-law in?'

The broker went into the adjoining room like a ghost. Maigret opened the door.

'Will you come in, Mademoiselle Nicole? Your brother-in-law won't be a moment.'

Suddenly he said:

'You don't wish to die?'

'No!'

'Good! Be careful...'

'Of what?'

'Nothing...Don't allow yourself to be dragged into...'

'What did he tell you?'

'He told me nothing.'

'Do you still think he's to blame?'

'You must ask him...'

'Where is he?'

Maigret had to turn his head to hide a smile.

'He's...recovering his wits!' he said.

And he re-lit his pipe which had gone out, while Voivin, like a man who is dazzled by the light, groped his way back into the office.

'Ferdinand!' Nicole cried.

'No! Not here ... PLEASE!' Maigret growled.

Rooftop over the Champs-Élysées

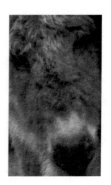

Roland Dorgelès

I live between two world-famous rivers; one has green water, the other, black tarmac: the Seine and the Champs-Élysées. From my eighth floor, I can see their rows of trees, and hear the rumbling of cars mingled with the hooting of tug-boats. Sometimes in the mornings military music makes me sit up and listen: troops marching up to the Arc de Triomphe for a ceremony; or, towards evening, a clamour and the sound of chanting: demonstrators clashing with the police. So I am the first to know about all the celebrations and all the riots; I can take the pulse of Paris without moving from my room.

But I didn't choose this opulent quarter where I've been living now for nearly thirty years. Apart from its trees and its wide streets, I didn't really care for it very much. There are some areas that are pensive, like the Sorbonne, or distressed, like Belleville, constantly on the move, like the Bourse, or free and easy like Montparnasse. The Champs-Élysées is distinguished only by its sense of propriety. You don't see any fruit and vegetable barrows there, nor any illegal street pedlars, the folk who make a street come alive. Its suspicious households keep their doors locked.

Nonetheless, having found nothing in Montmartre—the area I'd wanted to live in—I allowed myself to be seduced by an apartment perched high in the air where the noise couldn't reach me and, especially by a kind of pigeon-loft on the floor above, which I planned to make into my study. The room wasn't large, but it opened out on to a wide balcony where I could already picture myself watering the flowers and throwing seeds to the birds. That decided me. In short I rented something not mentioned in the terms of the lease: the silence and the sky.

Not many people know this area. They say: 'It's on the Champs-Élysées.' But don't believe a word of it! Our end has nothing to do with the famous avenue. We dwell modestly on the edge, more exactly between the Cours-la-Reine, the Place de l'Alma and the Rond-Point. Not even the Avenue Montaigne on the opposite side, where porters in stripes guard a large theatre and a luxury hotel, still belongs to us. We can still lay claim to the few discreet streets which are as yet unspoiled by neon lights and cinema queues.

Before the war they were even more like streets in the provinces. This provincial character was much to my liking. To put it more succinctly, I'd be living near the Concorde but feel at the same time as if I was a long way from Paris. Meanwhile the *quartier* has modernized, but fortunately not too much, and I am hoping it will keep one foot in the past for some time yet.

Actually, it's not even appropriate to call it a *quartier*. It would be better to say *parish*. It's a model parish in fact, for in a hundred metres there are four churches: the Armenian, the Italian, the Scottish and that of the Missionaries of the Assumption. Four radio stations (the same number as there are holy sanctuaries) have sprung up around the small Place François I, and the priests, the bearded *papas* and the clergymen are obliged to close their ears to the worldly tunes that escape from the windows; for their part, the presenters in their trousers and the young technicians in their check shirts remain unaware of their neighbours' psalms. Plainchant and jazz won't ever mix.

In the beginning I felt rather lost in this island of the bourgeoisie, I didn't belong there at all. But as soon as I went out, to my great surprise, I discovered memories everywhere. First, when I found the commemorative chapel built on the site of the Bazar de la Charité. Suddenly I could picture myself in short trousers, kneeling in front of an altar in the suburbs with my little friends praying for the victims of the fire in which 125 people, a royal personage and I don't know how many marchionesses and countesses, had perished. Unaware of the principle of charity sales, I thought that they were talking about a real bazaar, a shop full of toys and household items, and it surprised me that so many fine ladies had come to make their purchases there. I remember too that I was proud of knowing one of the rescuers, a typographer from the newspaper *La Croix*, who had snatched women from the blaze with their dresses on fire. Meanwhile gentlemen were beating their own way with canes through the screaming crowd to get to the exit. That vision was in my mind for a long time and when I walk past Notre-Dame-de-Consolation, I still recite two statistics out loud: 120 women and girls burned alive— and just five men, three of whom were elderly. Those fine gentlemen were faster on their feet…

Near there, on the opposite side of the road, were once shady trees in the garden of a wealthy mansion. The Germans cut them down to build an ugly blockhouse. Many years later it was removed but the cool of the ancient trees was never restored to us. Even in this opulent quarter we are not permitted the luxury of a public garden and the last big houses and stable yards are condemned to vanish.

The most charming of these old houses was on the corner of Cours-la-Reine, a small Renaissance mansion built formerly in Moret for Diane de Poitiers, then transported three centuries later to the banks of the Seine at the whim of another beautiful woman. They took it down carefully, stone by stone, to rebuild it in the small town where it came from in Napoléon's time, and replaced it with a high building which hides a bit more of the shady banks of the Seine.

All the roads in the neighbourhood hurried there to admire this priceless façade, and they must have been named in its honour: François I, Bayard, Jean Goujon ... From the little provincial square where they meet, around a dried-up fountain, you can see Montaigne going by, and on the other side, Clément Marot, Pierre Charron, Robert Estienne, La Trémoille approaching. Perhaps it was in homage to these illustrious forefathers that the architects from the middle of the last century adopted the Renaissance style, its mullioned windows and handcrafted pilasters. These romantic houses almost always ended under the pickaxe and the sledgehammer, but one that I love was saved—the one lived in by Victor Hugo. There is nothing to indicate this as you go by, yet it was here that he wrote *Notre-Dame de Paris*.

Often as I pass in front of his dwelling I look up at the little balcony on the first floor and expect him to appear there in his big grey woollen jersey. At the end of the day, attracted by the noise of little bells, he would break off from his writing and lean out to look at the goats which were coming back from the Champs-Élysées. Once the herd had passed he would half-close his eyes for a moment and the little goat-girl, moving off with her goats, was magically transformed into a gipsy girl from a fairy-tale in a gaily-coloured dress 'as thin and as lively as a wasp', followed by her little goat with the golden horns. I swear Esmeralda was born on this street.

I know why the Enchanter has stopped appearing at his window: the goats no longer come by. For more than a hundred years they followed this path that leads to the outskirts of Paris and until the war I too waited for the sound of the little goat bells before putting down my pen. But when, after four years away, I returned to Paris, I couldn't hear them any more. The street, previously deserted, was now too busy; and you can't hear the cab horses trotting, either, back to their stalls in the Rue Bayard. They demolished those too, and we shall no longer see the stable boys in baggy breeches crossing the street for a drink, nor the fresh-faced horsewomen laughing as they set off for the Bois.

The models from the fashion houses have taken their place but, although they are just as pretty, I do not think they are so attractive. Elegant without ostentation, scarcely made up, even more distinguished-looking than many of their clients, they can claim to be the queens of the *quartier*; their only fault is that they are too aware of it.

I see them some evenings getting into the sports cars of young gentlemen. They do it as confidently as if the car belonged to them. On other days they modestly take the metro, yet retain the same disdainful air. To look at them you would think they are going to catch *le Train Bleu*.

Their sempstress cousins and their neighbours, the typists, are not so alluring but are more lively. Hardly has the bell of Saint-Pierre-de-Chaillot finished ringing and they are off, chattering the while. One or two, darting a quick look towards the end of the road, satisfy themselves that *someone* is waiting and at the Rond-Point or Clemenceau leave the group, go round the Grand Palais, walk along by the Petit Palais, and when they have met up with him, vanish into the garden. The children playing around the kiosk have gone: at this time of day the groves belong only to the lovers.

Whenever I walk in that direction, I come across them under every tree, chairs pulled together, and I avert my gaze, afraid of being indiscreet. But I am quite wrong to worry: nothing disturbs them. Not the smiling passers-by nor the park keeper who has his eye on them, nor Monsieur Ticket who tries to make them pay, and if I pass by again a while later, I find them in the same position, legs twined together, lips still touching. Their kiss has to last the time of their rendez-vous.

Not that they realize, but it's traditional to embrace under the leafy shade of these trees, and the tradition is centuries old. Marie de Médicis, who had this path laid out to escape from the Louvre, herself jealously watched the pretty maids of honour around whom the beribboned courtiers flocked. In the days of the Sun King officers in plumed hats met their belles in frilly dresses; in the reign of Louis XV, coquettes in pannier dresses jumped out of their coaches into the arms of their lords in embroidered juste-au-corps. Later came the *merveilleuses* in their antique gowns, followed by dandies in long dress-coats and with ties up to the chin. Nothing changed except the costumes.

Before the Great War there was a mix of classes. Shy infantrymen in red trousers wooed large nurses in white caps, and amorous skaters, come from the Palais de Glace, watched for veiled ladies to appear. In spring young painters with open-necked shirts coming back from the Salon, proud of their first medals, dragged swooning models along those same paths; shortly before midnight it was the turn of the tipsy singing couples leaving the Jardin de Paris. Kisses, endless kisses.

Nowadays rich love-birds have found other places to escape to—in a car you can travel so fast—but the young working girls, the saleswomen, the typists don't go seeking happiness at such distances and the intoxicating music of the nearby *salon de thé* gives them the illusion of a love life among riches, in Venice or somewhere. Like film stars...

I have witnessed so many unimaginable events on this walk! At this very spot in 1910 I saw the raging Seine rise up over the parapet and its waters flood like a lake as far as the Chevaux de Marly; in the Avenue Montaigne I helped frightened girls cross the little bridges thrown for them by sailors in pompoms. Seagulls were fishing all around the Grand Palais and in some streets people were getting about in boats. You might think I made that up, but I saw it with my very own eyes!

However could I have supposed that I wasn't in any way attached to this area? I was in familiar territory. At the end of the Rue Alexandre I saw Clemenceau standing on his rock. 'Bonjour, patron!' I shouted to him gaily. (Ever since then I've got into the habit and never forget to say 'Hello' when I go by. He must be extremely bored...) His felt hat well down over his head, his bronze comforter flying, you would think he was off to eternity; but you know what?—he is well aware that our miserable eternity will not last long...

This statue tells me things it doesn't tell everyone. It reminds me that ever since my young days I was destined for the Champs-Élysées. Indeed, if the man who was not yet Father Victory took me on as a colleague just before the Great War, it was with the backing of an artist who had just become famous not far away. And what an exceptional artist! A donkey, nothing less! The one from the *Lapin Agile*, gentle Lolo, who became Boronali, whose picture I had exhibited at the *Salon des Indépendants* on the Cours-la-Reine.

Good old Lolo! It's to you I owe my 200 francs and the honour of having got nearer to this great man. And I for my part made you famous. So we are quits.

Nowadays the *Indépendants* are not relegated to fairground stalls. They are received in the Grand Palais like their old rivals the French artists, but both parties look like poor relations. The general public flocks only to the Motor Show or the Ideal Home Exhibition. You can get by without pictures, but not cars, televisions or washing-machines. In spite of which they have preserved a pompous inscription on the pediment, which I can make out as I am watering my plants: 'This monument was consecrated by the Republic to the Glory of French Art.' Some gift it was, to be sure, this cumbersome edifice! It is horrible, I'd like to knock it down! If it were not for its huge glass vault and slate domes I would be able to see the Louvre, Notre-Dame, the Sainte-Chapelle. They are what's missing from my horizon.

Now I've just had to accept it. What does it matter if a few spires are hidden? The Paris which stretches out before me holds so many marvels! Opposite is the Dôme des Invalides, its discreet gold reflects the rays of the sun; to the east, the Panthéon stamps its seal on the Montagne Sainte-Geneviève; to the west the Eiffel Tower rises up into the sky. Between them appear so many domes, cupolas, spires that I am confused by them. I mistake the Sorbonne for the Val-de-Grâce, I have trouble identifying Saint-Étienne du Mont, I look in vain for the Observatory, and the new block of the Faculty of Medicine half-hides the spires of Saint-Germain-des-Prés. On the other hand, the twin towers of Saint-Sulpice still look down upon their religious *quartier* and continue playing the flute up in the clouds. For a long time I thought them ugly; I am beginning to love them.

On this side of the Seine, the buildings are not so numerous; not so famous either. Only the Arc de Triomphe is worthy of admiration. The modern churches in my view are negligible: Saint Augustine's, la Trinité, Saint-Vincent-de-Paul. Either they are too luxurious or too austere. And I don't know what's inside those huge buildings with the rows of windows all over the place like filing cabinets. They must be waste-paper factories. I'd rather not know. In the mist I think I can make out the wooded slopes of the Buttes-Chaumont, but it may just be Père-Lachaise; on the other side I am unsure if it's Ville-d'Avray or Meudon.

Through the changing play of perspective the buildings approach one another. The cupola of the Opéra appears to be on top of the long green roof of the Madeleine, and Sainte-Clotilde is sloping down towards the Quai d'Orsay. And there's the steeple of Montrouge that I couldn't find before; there too are the Palais de Chaillot, the Salpêtrière, the gilded Pegasuses on the Pont Alexandre, the small dome of Dufayel. Well now, I've counted them all, there is nothing left. And yet... Notre-Dame, the Louvre, the Sainte-Chapelle... It's the accursed Palais that has spirited them away.

Luckily it has not hidden the Butte from my view. Modestly dressed in a cloak of grey houses it only has its white tiara as a distinguishing mark; no monument, no spire; nevertheless it's to that place I return. I discover charming little places that no one notices nowadays: shacks beribboned with honeysuckle, the vegetable gardens of convents, old wells with rusty chains, barrels from the taverns, an abandoned park, three mills, a thatched cottage. The backdrop to my youth now all gone...

This thought fills me with gloom. Why do I constantly have to remember how old I am? This evening I get no respite from Time. What's the matter with this old dummy that he pursues me, mumbling dates at me? If he thinks he can scare me, he's wrong! I think he is ridiculous with his false beard, his ceremonial scythe and his cumbersome hourglass. He can growl and threaten; I shan't listen, I don't give a damn about his advice, and even if it's cold I am determined to climb up there. It's Sunday today, everything will be lit up, I shan't miss the transfiguration.

At this hour another city appears. Less sumptuous in spite of being clothed in light, less prodigal with its riches. It has covered up its monuments in a black eiderdown and shows only the ones it is proud of: the Dôme des Invalides gloriously radiant, the Arc de Triomphe with its crystal halo, the Panthéon suddenly lit up, the showy Opéra, the Sacré-Cœur suspended in the air like an altar lamp and our tall, crazy Tower which makes an exhibition of itself, immodestly, beneath its lace chemise, its sides elongated and its legs splayed.

The world has turned into fairyland. On the esplanade the cars perform their silent ballet and the Grands Boulevards trace another Milky Way in the sky. Thanks to the flaming signs—red, blue, green—which are obscured and then reappear, I can find my way as though it were broad daylight. This moving pyramid, rising and falling, takes me to Place Clichy. Below that, the halo of Saint-Lazare; on the left the Ternes unfurl their streamers and over there behind me lie the illuminated hieroglyphs of Montparnasse. By straining my eyes I can spell out the adverts on the roofs; biscuits, aperitifs, mineral water, under-wear, tyres, cigarettes: the night offers a bit of everything on its street stalls. If I want to take flight, the magic carpet of the Champs-Élysées is at my feet. But I am not tempted by distant journeys. It's always Montmartre which draws me back.

Nothing stirs in the darkness surrounding the Sacré-Cœur. Only a practised eye can discern a pinprick of light on the top of the hill: the Moulin de la Galette. I used to live next to it... Taking my bearings from there, I embark on the climb, cross the Pont Caulaincourt, turn right up a steep slope and enter the Rue Lepic with my heart beating fast. I don't dare go any further. Too many memories lie in wait for me. But I am not avoiding them; I take a bitter delight in them.

Then it is that I feel as though a young boy has come and sat next to me, and his presence bothers me. In the darkness I can guess what he looks like: hollow cheeks, an ironic mouth, a rebellious curl pulled down over his forehead. I could tell you how old he is: scarcely more than twenty. And I know what he thinks... I shake him, to snatch him out of his reverie:

'Come on now, look somewhere else... feast your eyes on Paris instead, see how it sparkles... I give it to you, here, take it!'

But he doesn't listen. Sardonically, he bites his lips, a tic that I am all too familiar with, and I know full well he would not give up the small apartment he lived in over there for the luxurious balcony I have brought him to today.

The Cheeky Pigeon that Shat on People's Heads

Vincent Ravalec

He had been watching it for some time, the bird took off, described a graceful curve in the air so as to position itself above its target, and *wham*, after a little flutter of wings, relieved itself of its cargo onto the unfortunate person who happened to be there, the innocent victim of a fate meted out by a vindictive pigeon in the middle of Paris, in the Rue des Martyrs, a step or two away from the Place Pigalle and its cafés, *Aux Noctambules* and *La Nuit*.

The first time, he thought it was by chance, shit, did you see that, that pigeon just shat on that man's head, but as the bombardment happened a second time, he was obliged to conclude that it was not a question of an unfortunate accident but of a well-thought-out, consciously planned act of a bird mad for revenge, recklessly intent on war, and a clever enough strategist to squirt its ill humour on to a considerable number of passers-by every half hour.

They were discussing new scientific developments, combination therapies, and then mad-cow disease and the terrifying epidemic, the cows went mad, they slavered and teetered all over the place, their brains turned and became soft and spongy, this awful sickness was the result of something unbelievably scary, something that made your blood run cold, they had fed *meat* to cows.

But what's crazy is that just when they find a cure, some other thing starts.

He had nodded in silent agreement, a little way off a sandwich man coming from Anvers was shuffling towards them in the heat, and he thought the chap must be sweating blood, being a sandwich man in weather like this, the atmosphere was stifling, more than thirty degrees, he wouldn't like to be in his shoes.

There's no point going on and on about AIDS if as soon as they've found a cure they come across something else just as deadly.

This time he had been more positive, yes, that was certainly true, but were combination therapies really going to change anything, were people absolutely sure they worked? As he posed the question he could see a herd of cows advancing, teeth protruding from their drooling muffles, like vampires waiting to pounce, then attacking with their jaws sticking out and with wild, hooded eyes, mad cows, and behind them evil-looking cowboys astride their black mounts, horrifying herdsmen bearing poisoned meat, putrefying corpses they fed to the animals.

Of course it works—if they don't give all the treatment out to everybody it's because of the lolly, they want to keep it for the well-off, that's all.

At least with mad-cow disease you might suppose that it would still be democratic, the rich weren't the only ones who ate steak.

Sometimes he asked himself what on earth he was here for and what was the meaning of it all.

None.

Zilch.

Or there was a special significance.

Thousands of years he'd been coming back, and for what? Sometimes it was beyond him, he wondered what on earth to make of it.

Nothing.

Or there was a special significance.

I have been coming to this earth for thousands of years and my life has a *special significance.*

What are you thinking about? his mate asked anxiously. Don't you agree it's not fair them treating us like shit?

A group of teenagers were coming up the street again, shouting and screaming, the pigeon seemed to be considering the situation, coolly, weighing up the wind-speed and the cross-currents, then, no doubt thinking the conditions favourable enough, had taken off, flown over its young victims in a perfect arabesque and *splat*, had showered them with guana.

Even for someone of his experience, having lived thousands of successive lives, a remarkable journey through the ages of the world, this was a very rare sight.

A cheeky pigeon deliberately shitting on people's heads.

I dunno, perhaps they really didn't have enough medicine in the first place.

He'd been reincarnated as famous people, kings, great artists as well as down and outs. Pathetic old guys.

People like you and me.

People who might be susceptible to getting pigeon crap on their heads, ordinary people.

His mate had digested his answer while taking a swig of beer, cold beer they had bought at Shopi. I think you're completely wrong, I don't think you know what multinational drug companies are, they look after their own interests and those interests are more important to them than anything else.

Thinking about all the lives he'd lived, he felt rather weak, a faint fatigue.

Exactly, they are interested in selling drugs, not just getting rid of them.

The sandwich man looked exhausted, a tramp offered him a drink of coca cola and he accepted, mopping his brow, the message he was carrying read: 'Be prepared! Ouros is nigh.' That guy wasn't afraid of catching something, drinking from a tramp's bottle, he reflected, not everybody would have done that, perhaps he was immune, ignorant or protected by Ouros.

He tried to think if the name meant anything to him, Ouros, it was some kind of mythological business, Greek or Egyptian, but it was no good, nothing very definite came to mind.

The question that remained was what they were going to do with these cows. Killing them all would mean a colossal amount of work, killing them and then burning them, like a gigantic holocaust destined for some unidentified, unknown deity, who was stealthily invading the consciousness of the world, let's propitiate him or we are done for. The Ouros man was now very near, he had glanced briefly in their direction, there was room on the bench for one more, although with the board on his back it wasn't obvious he could sit down.

In any case, said his mate, it's a worry—for ten years I've been getting used to the idea that I'm going to kick the bucket, if the new medication really does cure you I'm going to have to change my mindset completely.

Yes, he said, yes, that's for sure unless of course we've been contaminated by mad-cow disease. The pigeon was slyly watching an old man coming down the street. He'd even been reincarnated as tyrants, monsters, one of his previous incarnations was high in the top ten of the most universally acknowledged bastards. What would be left of us once all that had gone, it was difficult to imagine.

Do you realize the number of people being considered now as potential stiffs, and who'll come back to life?

He'd repeated Watch out, watch out, don't be hoping for miracles, in case the new medication isn't a hundred per cent successful. The new medication lessens the strength of the virus but they don't know whether it will have a lasting effect or not. By the metro you could see the headlines of the newspapers on the sides of the booth. Seven monks had been bumped off in the Maghreb, he reflected that it was like the Seven Churches of the Apocalypse, the seven churches Saint John had written to. Had someone already had the idea of seeing the world as an equation?

$$\frac{(\text{Place Pigalle} \pm \text{combination therapies}^2 - \text{seven murdered monks})}{(\text{a vindictive pigeon})} +$$

$$\sqrt{(\text{people walking in the streets}^{10} + \text{the Apocalypse})} -$$
$$(\text{a feeling of fatigue and lights at night in the city}) \times Z = X$$

Yes, no doubt, no doubt, but that solved nothing.

Could I have a quick word with you about Ouros?

Ouros multiplied by the AIDS virus take away the added value of the average of seasonable variations, the whole lot divided by the number of lives lived on earth. Not long ago he had taken a taxi whose driver was convinced it was the devil who was in charge of the world, that he'd succeeded in taking power, and nobody had noticed, and at the time he'd replied in a distracted sort of way.

Ouros speaks of good and evil as of two things each necessary to the other, as reflection.

His friend said vamoose, eff off without even bothering to reply, but the chap did not give up but demanded to know what made them think Ouros wasn't a major subject worthy of interest.

I'm sceptical, he admitted finally, I'm naturally sceptical and anyway I don't believe in Ouros.

The chap went away up the Rue des Martyrs, the pigeon had flown over him without trying anything, Ouros creating around his agent perhaps an anti-shit aura. His mate re-lit the end of his rolled cigarette which had just gone out and they stayed there in the heat of the summer, quietly enjoying the noise, the petrol fumes and the passers-by, and the news of the day, like old men already rather tired, one full of hope about combination therapies but nevertheless worried when he realized he might lose his disability allowance, and the other one half mad, supposing himself reincarnated and thinking about the Apocalypse.

The Street is not Enough

Aurélie Filippetti

The houses press up one against the other along the ancient Roman road which leads from the old village of Saint-Marcel to the Montagne Sainte-Geneviève.

The thick bulk of their upper storeys absorbs part of the daylight.

There is a jumble of chimney stacks on the grey flaking roofs.

A café opens its windows on to the square. In the café, loud voices.

'I think it's all right!'

'You're joking!'

'It's very nice of you, but it's not going to be outside *your* house!'

'Where do you actually live?'

'Oh, in the Boulevard Saint-Michel, I see now. It's not next door to you, so it won't bother you.'

'In other words, it's none of your business.'

'If it was somewhere else we should still have a view, but not here.'

'You're free to think what you like but at least don't come preaching to us.'

'Please don't tell us what's right and wrong.'

'In any case it's not a question of what's right, but of the geography. You have to be realistic: the truth is, it doesn't seem to me to be the best place for it.'

'They could put it somewhere else.'

'That would be better for everybody.'

'Especially for them.'

'And for the tourists.'

'And for our kids.'

'Yes, because they are bound to bring their germs with them.'

'They'll be parking on the pavement, getting in the way of pedestrians.'

'Sleeping in their pools of vomit, being sick all over their shoes.'

'Being sick all over *our* shoes.'

'They'll just be there.'

'Everywhere you look.'

'We shan't be able to go out without seeing them.'

'If they come, I am going!'

'This is a family area.'

'There are other areas, we've chosen to live here.'

'And we've made a sacrifice…'

'Have they thought about the families?'

'We were fine here, it's family-friendly.'

'That's the reason we like this area, why we live here, why we feel all right.'

'It's quiet, that's why we are here.'

'If it changes, we're leaving!'

'Quite honestly, don't you think it's irresponsible?'

'We don't want them, no, we don't want any of that.'

'Who decided such a thing, I wonder.'

'Apparently they are going to bring them here from all over Paris, whole planeloads, and as they won't know where to go they'll come here for food and then they'll stay on.'

'And even from the *banlieue*.'

'It's not that I'm against helping them, not at all, but why not help them where they are—where they were staying up till now?'

'There's something set up already in the 15th.'

'Or in the 19th?'

'And even in the 13th, they certainly go to Austerlitz for soup, and that's a good thing.'

'Or else to Nanterre, after all, it's nearer their lodgings.'

'Yes, Nanterre's fine.'

'They've got everything they need over there.'

'Because you know, if you do too much for them, that's not helping them.'

'We have to encourage them to get out of their situation, not to do nothing.'

'Otherwise, it makes it too easy for them.'

'Nanterre is fine in any case, why can't they stay over there?'

'Since they've got nothing to do, why come to Paris?'

'They'd do better to look for work.'

'It's too dear here, there's nothing for them.'

'It's not doing them any favours putting them in places like this. They haven't got the price of a cup of coffee, you know.'

'We're being reasonable, we pay our rent, that's not for nothing. What's the point otherwise?'

'We take our kids to school every morning.'

'It's dangerous.'

'The kids mustn't see them, they'd be scared.'

'What are we going to tell the kids?'

'And then there's the germs…'

'Germs?'

'Yes, germs, viruses, bugs, dirt, smell, the look of them.'

'The universities are just opposite. We just can't.'

'The students won't agree to it.'

'The students' parents won't agree to it.'

'The Rector of the university is not in favour.'

'No, Paris isn't the place for it. Paris can't play host to all the poor in the…'

'They say it's lodging for families, a roof for people who don't have one, a place for them to eat, a temporary shelter when it's cold outside or too hot on the pavement, but isn't the street enough for them, then?'

'They do nothing all day, so of course they'll hang around, they'll put down roots, they'll make themselves at home, and it'll be cosy here, they won't want to leave, it's so comfortable in this district.'

'They'll be pestering us for money all the time, soon as you leave your house they'll have their hands out, and you can give to this one or that one but you reach a certain point where you just can't any more!'

'You already see them when you come out of church on Sundays, after Mass, there are more and more. Of course they know very well it's the best place.'

'Not stupid, are they!'

'I've been listening to you for the last ten minutes. Well, I'll tell you something. Let me tell you what happened to me. It will be more revealing than long speeches. Everyone should know how it happens. What has happened and what will happen. We're fed up with blather. I'll tell you this for real: last year I was on my way home. It was early evening, not even dark. I was walking along quietly, I used to give a euro now and then when I could. But no more! I'm not saying some are not okay, they can't help it. They're clean, at least, and don't make a noise. But it's not like that any longer. I was attacked, Monsieur. Yes, attacked, I was going home, doing no harm to anybody. There were two guys. They came up. One asked me for a cigarette. And then he told me to give him some cash, or else. He slapped my face—a slap, yes. And threatened me. I went to the doctor and got five days off work. It frightened me to death. I thought I'd have a breakdown. That's what goes on in the districts where they house people like that. You can't do that in the middle of Paris. You really can't. Look at what happened to me. Well, that's what it's like nowadays, so as for me, I don't want them. Full stop. We work all day and even weekends, but at least let's be safe in our homes! I don't do politics, you know. They're all the same to me. I don't give a damn for all that. But what happened to me tells you something. That's what life is like today, so forget about your speeches. And don't let them tell us the house has been unoccupied for ages, that's true, but all the same. They could have done something else with it.'

'It's true that since that block was left empty, at least they have done up the outside, it's nicer now, you've got to admit.'

'The previous owner was way out of order too. The price she was asking for her small flats. Students who weren't even French, they went back home and she never even gave them their caution money back.'

'At least today it's clean.'

'Yes, but for how long?'

'How many rooms have they made out of it? There are going to be a lot of people.'

'Apparently there will be families as well as single people and a big dining room.'

'That building was nearly falling down. The *patron* of the *bistrot* opposite was always afraid one day a piece would come away and fall on his head.'

'Now they've restored it. And it's true, in spite of everything the street seems brighter.'

'Perhaps, but when I think of the trouble we all take…'

(whispering) 'Do you know they had to carpet the whole place?'

'Oh, why?'

'I don't know. Usually people prefer wood floors, but in this case the workmen told me they'd been told to cover all the wood with carpet in the family flats.'

'Because of the kids. They say they're afraid of anything in wood these days.'

'And especially that they mustn't have a fireplace.'

'So they have to avoid anything that might remind them of…'

'No gas heaters either.'

'Not the slightest flame.'

'They are afraid of fire.'

'That's quite understandable, isn't it.'

Rue Pigalle

Francis Carco

I never climb the Rue Pigalle at night without remembering how, going home through the dark streets as a small child, I would turn round at every step, to look at the very brightly-lit merry-go-rounds which—the further off I went—shone ever brighter. It was as if they were bidding me farewell. Beneath the grey winter sky, between the trees with their small bare branches, a pink and greenish luminescence slanted very sharply through puffs of steam and smoke and this play of light, the last thing I saw, was a source of great pain to me.

Then with a heavy heart I had to climb the damp staircase of our damp house, leave my sorrows on the threshold, resign myself, put it out of my mind, even dry my tears on occasion, and in my little bed comfort myself as best I could.

Cœur d'enfant, cœur d'enfant, que tu me fais de la peine!

So Bataille lamented, a man to whom heartbreak was a familiar visitor. My pain was acute. Yes. And it lasted. It still lasts and hurts even now, if I let it, because in the provinces when the bottles and jars of the pharmacies cast their magical lights across the streets, the fair with its thousands of revolving lamps, its noise and its music, made my head spin. I could never get enough of it. Despite the rain, even if there was only one single stall with twenty or so people under its waterlogged canvas, I would rush to it, I swelled the number of curious onlookers, I revelled in its astonishing delights. How can I best convey the strange sensations that took possession of me, open-mouthed amongst so many wonders? No use me trying. However carefully I chose my words, and tried my hardest to communicate the sense of excitement that pervaded me then, I should never succeed. And besides, 'words and more words...a sorry game!'

* * *

Even today in the Rue Pigalle, if I happen to be going home late, I turn round every step of the way to look at the lights. I look at the customers in the big cafés who come and go as they please, and, like the child that I was, I have a kind of ache when I tell myself that, of all those people there, I'm the one who has to go to bed first. Is it only for them that Paris switches on its milky-white footlights every night, the pink and blue lettering on its tall publicity signs, its streamers of electric lights, and spreads out all over the pavement under the women's artificial smiles something that looks like a silken carpet? Jazz from all sides, it drifts down the streets, crosses to and fro, rises drumming and singing up the pale façades where the brilliant lights of the luminous signs seem to flicker in time to its shimmying rhythm.

Delicious moment! Somewhat intoxicated, you are borne along, emboldened, guided steadily towards that secret loving fairy princess of your dreams who, imprisoned by bourgeois prejudice, only appears to humans after great effort, after long searching. She it is who, in a flash of light, fixes you with the vacant and abstracted look of a stranger; who halts then and follows another passer-by, not you. She who deserved better, or worse. Do we know which? Don't ask her for an answer. Her charms would immediately dissipate and you would hear her say in a husky, broken voice, in sardonic tones, 'Are you coming with me, darling?'

* * *

Oh, how disappointing it is, even elsewhere than in those cosy little houses that so abound in Paris, to discover the dark side of pleasure! You have to be wary of that in the Rue Pigalle. You don't need to do more than look, the look's enough. Her make-up, her perfume, her artfulness, her fleeting accent. Here in a bar with a chalky ceiling and white globes, seeing negroes reminds you of the seedy dives in ports. There in the narrow alleyway of a very famous impasse, is a house with closed shutters. Higher up towards the fountain and its feeble jet, towards the square chock-a-block with buses, Cossacks from Tbilisi in jackets of such a pale blue it looks like a thin, fragile layer of pastel, show you their long daggers. The veiled shop windows, the clusters of lights, the *bistrots* with a soft steam on the mirrors, the entrance halls carpeted in deep velvet, create such a décor that poor old people with empty haversacks, newspaper vendors, weary flower-girls, feast on them, and ask the police the time, and wait for it to be too late for them to keep the appointments they have made.

At dawn when the multicoloured lightbulbs grow pale, there is a great to-do everywhere in the bars. Quite unprepossessing women tell you their troubles. They are like little orphaned girls who against this background of revelry tell you how tiring their job is and admit they would love to go to sleep. Some dream of their menfolk, who in prison are counting the days they are away from them. Others, foul-mouthed, pick quarrels with other girls. Not one now asks the price she thinks she is worth. On the contrary. They have a rare abandon which lets you approach them and gives you a sudden insight into what they are really like.

* * *

One of these 'young ladies' let me buy her a drink the other night, declaring:

'Give my money to some chap? Not on your life. Nothing doing. The man who'd get it off me hasn't been born.'

'Why's that?'

'Because I've got a kid and I work for her. I'm a dancer. And so...Oh! No, I tell you...I'm not about to let it go. My word I'm not! There might be one or two who'd try, but I wouldn't advise them to. They'd soon find out.'

She had just finished declaiming these words when an ugly, gloomy-looking puny fellow, who, wanting to look stylish, wore his cap as flat as a pancake, came over and addressing himself to my companion said:

'Madame, you are nothing but a bitch.'

'It's possible,' the girl responded.

'It's certain,' replied the young man.

So when I touched his elbow and asked him, 'What are you drinking?' he deigned to sit down and curtly ordered:

'A coffee laced with rum.'

In front of this gentleman the dancer seemed to me a little abashed. She lowered her eyes. But he looked me all over and enquired:

'Are you with Madame?'

'As you see.'

He shrugged.

'Well, y'know, as far as work goes, you've got a bad deal. She's a dead loss...And argumentative...And empty-headed.'

'What? What?'

This was 'Madame' who, not allowing such remarks at her table, was getting cross.

'Wait,' said our simple companion simply.

He summoned the waiter, got him to pour into another glass the rum which was going to lace his coffee, and seizing the glass, threw its boiling-hot contents in the poor girl's face, adding:

'Now, get lost, Madame. You are no friend of mine. Go away! Vamoose! As for your money, I tell you, out of the goodness of my heart—keep it! Neither Monsieur (he did me the honour of treating me as his equal) nor me, are short of a cent or two. Do you understand?'

'Oh, Alfred!'

'Don't Alfred me!'

'Yes!' the dancer protested jumping up, and wiping her face, drew nearer the ugly little fellow. 'Listen to me!'

'I'm not listening.'

'Look,' she said. 'Have you gone crazy or something? Alfred? What's the matter with you? You only make things worse...I'm going to get you another coffee.'

'No, Madame.'

But he was weakening. He couldn't resist the offer of another coffee that this humble girl standing in front of him, close to him, was offering so good-naturedly...And little by little, I saw him drop his defences and regain his composure. Then, very calmly, he said:

'Come on now, give me a little kiss first. Here...'

He pointed to his cheek.

'Come on now, a little kiss.'

The girl leaned over and silently bit him, hard, and he, so as not to show that she had hurt him, forced a laugh, while magnanimously hugging his girl and explaining:

'It's not that I really care for her. But when you've trained a woman up...you can't refuse her anything.'

Le Petit Parisien

CINQ CENTIMES

4ᵉ Année · N° 1196 · Nouvelle Série · N° 128

Supplément Littéraire Illustré

Dimanche 7 Janv

CINQ CENT

L'AUDACIEUSE AGRESSION DE LA RUE ORDENER

En pleine rue, en plein jour, des bandits, après avoir assailli et dévalisé un encaisseur peuvent s'enfuir en automobile.

Fol L⁴c 3850⁴

Hold-up in the Rue Ordener

Colette

There's something going on over there… Farther off, beyond the crowd of people who have been prevented from moving forward by a barrier of police and Paris guards; they spread in unequal streams over both sides of the road like long stagnant black pools… Behind the thick silica dust flying around like spume on waves… There's something going on over there, on the right side of the street, something everyone is looking at and nobody can see…

I've just arrived. In order to get to the front I've used brute force, like a woman at the sales in a department store, combined with the soft blandishments of the weaker sex: 'Monsieur, please let me through… Oh, I can't breathe, Monsieur… You are so lucky to be tall like that…' They let me go to the front because in this throng there are hardly any women. I touch the blue-uniformed shoulders of a policeman—one of the pillars of the crush barrier—and I try to move forward a little more:

'Monsieur l'agent…'

'You can't go through!'

'But those people running over there, look, you've let them through.'

'Those men are journalists. And anyway they are men. Even if you were from the press everybody in a skirt must stay quietly over here.'

'Perhaps Madame would like my trousers?' a voice from the *faubourgs* suggests.

Everyone laughs loudly. I bite my tongue. I look at the street barricaded with intermittent whirlwinds. I am focusing, like everybody, on an almost invisible point behind the dust and the curtain of trees: a grey shack of a building with its roof at an angle…I jig around, in agitated curiosity:

'What's going on? What have they done about it? Where are *they*?'

The policeman, his eyes on the street, doesn't answer. My neighbour, a woman with a lot of hair and protecting a child with each arm, looks me up and down. I turn on the charm:

'Tell me, Madame, are *they* over there?'

'The robbers? Oh yes, Madame. In that house over there.'

Her tone is clearly: 'Where have you sprung from? Everybody knows that!' A large fellow at my back coolly informs me:

'They are inside. The police are afraid they might escape so they are going to blow them up...'

'Blow them up? Oh, my word! I'll bet a tenner they get away and leave Lépine high and dry.'

This sporting remark comes from a pale blasé young man who can't keep still: shiftily he presses against the people around him, pushes against me as if by accident. I wager that he'll put his head down at the first opportunity, dive under the arms of the policeman and sprint up the empty street...

They are over there... They are going to be blown up... The dreadful mindset of the curious onlooker takes hold of me, the same which makes women go to bullfights, boxing matches and even to the foot of the guillotine, that spirit of curiosity which so perfectly makes up for a want of true courage... I dance around, bend my head to protect myself from the clouds of dust...

'Madame, if you think it's easy to see anything standing next to someone as fidgety as you!'

It's the mother, the stern woman by my side. I mutter something at her and she says tartly:

'But it's true! What's the point of me being here since nine this morning just so you get in front of me at the last moment? If people save a place, they save a place. And anyway, if you have a great hat like that, you take it off!'

She bossily holds out for her place in the front row and seeks—gets—general approbation. Behind me I hear a chorus of 'Take your hat off!', jokes which date from last year's vaudeville, but which leave a funny taste in the mouth when you remember what's going on over there…

All of a sudden the wind throws at us, with the dust that crunches between our teeth, the familiar smell, that distinctive smell of burning: over there it's no longer the dust which is blinding the street but the greyish blue of a smoke churned up by the wind… The shouts behind me rise like flames:

'They're there! They're there! Can you hear? I heard a shot! The house has been blown up! No, it's gunshots! They're getting away! They're getting away!…'

Nobody has seen or heard a thing, but this excitable crowd pressing on me from every side is inventing, without realizing it, perhaps telepathically, all the goings-on over there. Pressure has built up and now, irresistible, a surge breaks through the barrier and carries me forward. I am running so that I won't be crushed; I run with my neighbour and her two agile children. The sporty, blasé young man shoves me aside with his shoulder, a thousand are coming along behind. We run, with a noise like a herd of animals, towards the goal, ever more invisible: *over there*.

There is a sudden halt, then people run back, half knocking me down. On my knees I hang on to two solid arms which at first shake me hard and then pull me up. I haven't time to say thank you.

'Where are *they*? Where are *they*?'

A rather puny working woman in a black apron gasps:

'They've gone! They've escaped! Everybody's after them!'

She can't possibly know, she's seen nothing. She shouts, she's telling everyone what she has imagined. The throng drags us both along and lifts us up. I take shelter for a moment against a very tall man who lets himself be jostled and shaken without turning a hair, his two arms lifted and holding up a camera which he is blindly and incessantly pointing...

The dust, the smoke are suffocating... While the wind shifts the cloud covering us, I realize I am very near the building collapsing noisily in flames. But all at once the crowd carries me away and I am struggling not to be crushed... Confused cries; the voices are hoarse and throaty like sobbing. A shout is heard clearly, spreads and gives some coherence to all this uproar: 'Kill them! Kill them!' I can breathe again, thanks to a gap in the crowd...

'Kill them, kill them!'

And once more I am pushed, bruised, shoved up against the back of a motor car that is being opened to heave up into it *something* heavy, long and inert...

None of those shouting near me and around me can make out what is happening. But they are shouting because it's contagious, imitating others, almost, I might say, because they think it's the right thing to do.

That fair-haired quarryman yaps, mechanically, staring straight ahead. 'Kill them!' shouts a plump southerner in a guttural voice, and from his tone you would think he was saying: 'Exactly!' or crying 'Encore!' at a café-concert. I stare in amazement at two shopgirls, arm in arm and as jolly as at the Foire de Neuilly, who let themselves be pushed and shoved and jostled along and only stop shrieking 'Kill them!' to burst into giggles...

Between the heads, between the moving shoulders, I can see the ruined building with flames licking up around it. A man leans out of a smashed window and throws a mattress on the ground, the sheets soaked in so much blood, pink in the midday sun, that it seems to me artificial.

'Kill them!'

The violence and fury of the shouting is increasing! I feel the motor car slowly shudder and begin to move. I must once again run if I don't want to fall under the feet of people following it. As it drives off it seems to draw the whole crowd along with it like a magnet.

Finally I can slow down and stop. The automobile and its screaming escort vanish into the distance like a black stormcloud. Already the white road to the centre of Paris is covered by a yelling multitude, still half ignorant of what was in the midst of them. Breaking away from the main body of the crowd, I remain for some time looking at the cluster of flames fed by the dried wood, magnificent, joyous, shifting in the wind. So that's where *they* had gone to ground ...

Just a speck in the crowd, oppressed and blinded only a little while ago, I begin to see clearly again. It's my turn to go off into Paris and find out what dramatic event I have just witnessed.

2 May 1912

The Tree with Three Branches

Gisèle Prassinos

Night was descending on the houses in the Rue Tronchet. At the window of one of these buildings, two dark-skinned women, with very long hair and green eyes, were cutting up some red cloth which was falling in tiny pieces under the scissors. The hair of one of the women was encircled with a green ribbon which exactly matched her eyes. The other had hands that were whiter and wasn't wearing a ribbon but her eyes were covered in grey, opaque skin that disappeared into the back of her eyelids. They continued their work until from inside the apartment came a moaning, a voice of suffering like that of a lost soul. Then they got up quietly, leaving behind their cloth and scissors. They disappeared at the same time, with the same movement. After a moment the window banged shut and they were seen no more.

Night came and a bare arm closed the shutters. All went dark. No light lit up the street.

Towards midnight from that window came a long-drawn-out and chilling scream. Immediately multitudes of small red squares flew into the air. One by one they landed on the pavement below and the dirty water of the gutter carried them away. They vanished into a black hole at the end of the street.

* * *

At dawn, a man with his head bare, and only a rag around his waist, was walking slowly on the banks of the Seine. He was dragging by a string a large aluminium tin filled with a few bits of rubbish. Arriving under an arch, he sat down on the surface of earth and gravel. His naked body leaned against the cold and he smiled. This smile lingered on his soft, violet cheeks. His hollow eyes, like a blind man's, were turning around in their sockets and finally fixed on a distant object which floated on the waters of the river. It was something red, a shapeless mass of blood. A severed hand, livid in colour, was digging its nails into the soft matter, which was changing shape.

It floated by.

The water came.

Another thing went by: long black strings, strands of hair. The breeze skimming the water touched the hair lightly and turned it over.

The man saw a white ball pierced by two grey holes.

While day gradually dawned, the ball sank into the water, slowly, with the black strands following...

Rue de la Vieille Lanterne

David Constantine

1

That night his voice came up out of him, chanting and singing very loud, so that before long, for the good of the other inmates, an attendant entered and conducted him downstairs to a more secluded room, and locked him in. There his dream continued. He suffered it. The room had eight walls, he stood at the centre, turning to follow the images as they appeared, clockwise, on each. He saw all the beauty he had ever seen in his life before, but it was hacked, mutilated, piecemeal, and below it, written in blood in an Eastern script he could read with ease, the interminable chronicle of the world's violence writhed. And he knew: I am being shown this because I am responsible.

Dr Blanche came in. It was daylight, the everyday light. Blanche wore his everyday good nature and carried a cup of coffee and a brioche on a silver platter. Eat, he said. Drink. Then I should like to introduce you to a person whom you may perhaps be able to help.

He led him to the garden room, which was also the surgery. There in an armchair, two attendants standing by, sat a young man. His feet were bare, very white and shapely, his hands lay quietly in his lap, his eyes were closed, a length of rubber tube dangled from his right nostril. Nerval thought him as beautiful as a fallen angel. He was a soldier, said Blanche. He was in Africa. Now he won't open his eyes or speak. Nor, so far as I can tell, does he hear any sound. Worse still, he will not eat or drink. So we feed him liquid chocolate through a tube.

Nerval was transfixed. The mute soldier seemed to him another self, a younger brother, who had pushed on with the quest, to the final door, and sat there now, beyond the world's interferences, at the very mouth of God, listening. He will help me, he said aloud. Blanche shrugged. One another. Who knows? Then he withdrew, signalling to the attendants that they should follow him. The garden room shone with the light from outside.

Nerval kneeled before the soldier and took hold of his feet, which were cold. In such proximity he felt himself to be bulky, almost gross, the young man seemed slimmed in body and spirit for the crossing over. He contemplated the shut eyes, the closed, tightly pursed, lips, took the hands, also cold, and pressed them to his forehead, desiring a transfusion. No good, not close enough. He stood up, fetched a chair, seated himself so close that his and the soldier's knees interfitted, and bowed his forehead so that it pressed against the bowed forehead of the man who had escaped the empire of the senses. And in that posture, conjoined (so to speak) with a twin at the brows, Nerval began to whisper the chronicle of himself, the recurrent episodes of his suffering, the exaltations, the wanderings, the need for asylum, the need for flight, and his fear of the freezing that would come to him again soon, as it did every winter, from the river in Silesia which his dying mother had crossed when she was twenty-five. He felt assured that this presentation of his life passed with no diminution of its truth out of his brain into the young man's brain, through their brows; and that although he uttered it in words it passed not as words but as the current and pulse of them, from soul to soul. He had no sense of any passage of time, and was astonished when Dr Blanche came in and said it was noon, the soldier must have his semolina, and he, Nerval, was invited to table with himself, the physician, and two or three others among the patients whose conversation might be amusing and of interest.

That night Nerval dreamed such a dream that when he woke his face was wet with tears of joy. He had seen the soldier, or his double, in the other world, they were walking together in open country under a sky blazing with stars. They halted, the young man touched the older man on the forehead, addressed him as 'brother', and opened his eyes, they shone under the stars as though in daylight and their colour was periwinkle-blue. Nerval took a stick of charcoal and on one of the very few remaining spaces on the walls of his cluttered room he wrote: Last night you came to me.

Blanche mentioning that the soldier was a countryman, Nerval broke off the chronicle of his own ordeal and, still holding the patient's hands, still brow to brow with him, in a slow murmur he began to sing. Day after day then, for hours at a time, he sang the ancient songs he had collected from the Valois, his native land: love songs, elegies and ballads, in many different voices, the whole stock, beginning again wherever he pleased, remembering more, steeping himself in the country, its three sacred rivers, its countless haunted springs, still waters, deep forests, its festivals, struggles and sufferings, so many named places, so many named persons. He stood outside the door of the garden room until Blanche opened for him and let him in. The attendants were wiping the last drops of chocolate or semolina from the dangling length of tube, they removed the bib, arranged the young man comfortably, bare-footed, eyes closed, lips tight shut, the quiet hands folded in his lap. Left alone then, Nerval fetched his own chair, sat close, bowed the soldier's head to meet his at the brow, and softly and slowly began to sing.

So this intercourse continued until the first day of October, the trees in the garden—acer, hazel, beech— flaming in the colours of their dying, and on that day came the breakthrough. Leaning back from the young man, Nerval fixed his eyes on the shut mouth and sang:

> *Aux quatre coins du lit*
> *Des bouquets de pervenches*
> *Et nous y dormirons*
> *Jusqu'à la fin du monde…*

The soldier's lips moved. Nerval paused, watched them closely, sang the four lines again. Waited. Again the lips moved, but this time in obedience to the larynx, the tongue, the palate, the teeth, to make words. Quite without expression, as mere repetition and very softly, the soldier said:

> *Et nous y dormirons*
> *Jusqu'à la fin du monde.*

Nerval shuddered. It battered him like Pentecost. He exulted. After long absence he felt himself chosen once again to be the servant of the Good Angel, to raise a fellow sufferer out of torpor, to enable him to partake again of the life that had gone missing. Informed, Blanche nodded. Good, he said. You will help one another.

The following days strengthened this hope. Nerval sang a quatrain, stared hard at the young man's lips until they stirred and performed a repetition. From that, under Nerval's tuition, before and after the singing, these lips progressed to the exchanging of simple courtesies. Next, for one second, shocking his companion with ineffable joy, the soldier opened his eyes: they were periwinkle-blue, alien, like those of some lost and future race of human beings. A day or two later he opened them as any person might, looked around him, spoke unprompted a sentence now and then—all, it must be admitted, the looking and the speaking, without expression. He addressed Nerval familiarly, called him brother, without gratitude or wonder, simply as fact, they were intimates of longstanding, so it seemed. Still, of his own volition, he would not eat.

After the feeding, Blanche allowed them to walk in the garden for a while. They walked arm in arm, saying very little, or they sat side by side on a bench. Once, very beautifully, a blackbird sang, which Nerval brought to the soldier's attention and he nodded. Then he said, I am thirsty. Please will you fetch me a glass of water. Nerval obliged, handed it to him, he raised it to his lips, but could do no more than that. He seemed to own neither the idea nor the art of drinking. Yet he said again, in a vague distress, I am thirsty. Nerval took the glass from him. Why is it, he asked, that you cannot eat or drink? It is because I am dead, said the young man. I died a year ago in Mortefontaine. I am buried there. Nerval said, If that is so, where do you believe yourself to be now, at this moment, with me, here in this garden? Where do you think you are now? In Purgatory, said the soldier. I am in the process of my expiation.

Next morning, unshaven, half-dressed, white spittle at the corners of his mouth, Nerval entered Dr Blanche's consulting room unbidden and demanded to be released. It was, he said, quite intolerable that he should be incarcerated one day longer. He was a man of letters, he had commissions, obligations, which he could only fulfil at liberty in the city. By what right do you confine me here among the mad? Blanche spoke soothingly to him, bade him be seated. He was making good progress, soon, soon he would be well again. I beg you, my dear friend, let us not undo the good we have done. Be patient, let us have faith in one another. But Nerval could not be quietened. He stood up, paced to and fro, muttering to himself and clenching and unclenching his fists. Inspirations come to me, he said, and I cannot rightly hear them. I am being harmed in this bedlam. I demand my release. I wish to be among my own kind in the outside world.

For two days, uncouthly, Nerval put his demand to Blanche, in the end threatening him with a judicial process if he did not accede to it. Blanche was grieved. Father and son, Esprit and Émile, over many years, in Montmartre and Passy, they had cared for him, coaxed him out of the pit, out of the terrors in his head, enabled him to write again and to be his gracious self among his countless friends. The injustice wounded him, the son, as it had in the past the father. Very well, he said. Find two competent persons who will certify that they understand you wish to leave here against my professional advice and who support you in your wish nonetheless. I cannot be held responsible for any bad consequences. Further, I must have from someone who knows you well a promise to accommodate you for as long as may be necessary. Once I have those documents, you will be free to leave my house.

By the evening of the following day Jules Janin, a journalist, and Louis Godefroy, a lawyer, had written the letters Blanche asked for. And next morning from Mme Alexandre Labrunie, Nerval's aunt, came the offer of a room in her house at 54 Rue de Rambuteau for as long as he liked. Shortly before noon that day, 19 October 1854, Nerval left his doctor's house, 17 Rue de Seine, carrying only a battered valise and promising to have the contents of his room sent on after him very soon. He wore the famous black *redingote* of the many pockets, all of them stuffed full with books and work in progress. He looked aged, corpulent, altogether unsteady. Embracing Blanche, he began to shake with sobs. My dear Gérard, said Blanche. Think again. But he would not. He shrugged, as though it had to be. Turned and shambled like a bear the short distance to the *quai* and there boarded the omnibus just leaving for Paris, Place du Palais-Royal. He lived all his remaining days and most of his remaining nights on the city's streets.

2

The problem was not lodgings. He had friends all over Paris who at any hour of the day or night would have welcomed him in. Two or three women kept a room ready and waiting just for him, kept it clean and neat, with a desk to write at, and always a vase of flowers changing as they came in their seasons to the market, a room that was light and airy, with little amenities, touches they knew he would like. His friends had an image for him: he was the bird, the swallow, who flits in at the window left open for just that entrance, and rests, and flits out again, vanishing. He was not Jesus Christ: always within walking distance, Nerval had where to lay his head.

Nor was money the problem. He boarded the omnibus to Paris in stained and crumpled trousers, his coat, kerchief, battered *chapeau claque* might have been a huckster's, his shoes were down at heel and leaked at the soles.

But he wore the ring of Isis on the second finger of his left hand, he could have pawned it for clothes fit to appear in at any ball. He got money easily: whatever he wrote, the best journals and reviews would publish it, and they paid well. True, when he had money he got rid of it blithely, no friend ever asked and was refused, and to strangers also, if their plight moved him, he gave with both hands. But scores of men in Paris were in his debt, all would have repaid him with interest for some past kindness.

Neither money nor a lodging was the problem.

Swallow—or swift? He was likened to both. Both are waited for and when they come in on the winds of spring their arrival surprises like a thing that, after all, it was beyond us to imagine. The city loves them around her towers, steeples and attics. The streets, deep down, are glad of them above in the free air. They are travellers, they divide their year into hemispheres. A swallow might well land on your sill, look in, bide a while. But a swift never would, never could. Once launched, once evicted from the nest, they cannot land. They live in the air, they hunt and mate in the air, they ride its invisible pathways, they sleep on spirals down, down, and wake before they crash. The swift, *apus apus*: 'footless'.

He frequented various reading rooms, one under the south arcade in the Place des Vosges. There especially, they let him be. He read the journals, or sat quite abstracted, or wrenched a wad of tightly written pages out of an inside pocket and worried at them. At some point during any visit he would ask politely for a few sheets of paper. None who attended him ever forgot. Among the testimonies is this: I gave him the sheets, he thanked me with excessive courtesy, and from my desk on the far side of the quiet room I watched, I was ashamed to, but I did. I remember it now with fear and pity. He was sweating and his hands were shaking. He laid the sheets in a neat pile on the right, took up his pen, sobbed like a man breaking into pieces, and began. I saw him quieten, in that public room, I saw what it was like in him when for a space, in another respite, he wielded his pen against collapse. He wrote steadily, never pell-mell, with an unhurried certainty. His trembling ceased, on his face when he paused, looked up, waited to see the shape of a sentence and to feel for its rhythm, in his expression during those moments there was—forgive me this language—something seraphic. He looked conscious of his blessing, of his *being able*—which is why I should not have looked, I should have looked away, attended to my registers, but I did look, I watched, I couldn't help myself and now I can't regret it. I saw a man in the possession of his gift, doing what he was born to do, near the brink with no diminution of his powers, but near the end, near the ruin. He wrote, and I have read: I must command my dream, not suffer it. Still now in the light of afterwards

I see him in the public reading room for the last interlude doing precisely that.

He wrote in reading rooms, in cafés, in the rooms of friends. In the cold of that coldest winter for many years he wrote in churches, in their pews, on their steps, he wrote on benches in the public gardens and the cemeteries. And when he was not writing he was walking. Head crammed with the matter of his writing, he walked the streets, never idly, never strolling. Afterwards, many could remember seeing him and could tell you where—on the corner of the Rue Malebranche and the Rue Saint-Jacques, crossing the Pont du Carrousel, by the west door of Saint-Merri—and all agreed, if he saw you he would return your greeting, if you collared him he would bide politely as long as you held him, but in truth he was never at leisure, on the streets he had to keep moving, he looked hunted, some said, others said hunting, he looked hunted by or hunting after certain very compelling phenomena that nobody else could see. He saw the English girl on the steamer from Marseilles. She was biting into a lemon. He perceived that she was consumptive and would not live long. He saw her in the sea at Naples, she was swimming towards him, she vanished, rose again and stood with the water up to her small breasts, smiling, pleased with herself, and offering him on the platter of her outstretched hands a golden fish. The last time he saw her was at Herculaneum. He was underground, staring at the girl Proserpina with flowers on her left arm, staring and staring until he felt the cold draught of the Underworld on the nape of his neck, the hairs stood up, he turned and saw the white-faced English girl in the costume of Proserpina biting into a lemon with her small sharp teeth. And his mouth filled with the clear bitter juice as though it welled up from his beating heart. Turning into the Rue Basses-des-Carmes, he saw his way blocked by the possessions he had left in his room in the house of Dr Blanche. It was Faust's study, tipped out, all the mouldering tomes, the filthy alembics, all the learning in a jumble that made no sense, the sum total clutter to date, all the reading, all the bric-à-brac, all the souvenirs of travel in Europe and the East, there piled high, so that he could not proceed further down the narrow street. It was the condition the Illuminati call the *capharnaüm*, lumber-room, mêlée in the brain, bedlam. He blundered into a café, asked for cognac and some writing paper and wrote to Dr Blanche. He addressed him as 'dear friend', begged his forgiveness, and beseeched him to burn the contents of his room. But at once erased that sentence and instead, detailing every item he could bring to mind, asked that each be sent to the person whose name he set next to it. Thus:

A Florentine console supported by a winged sphinx: Alexandre Dumas

An eighteenth-century bed with a baldequin of red lampas: Jenny Colon

A narghileh from Constantinople: Heinrich Heine
Panelling from the Rue Doyenné: Théophile Gautier
A pilgrim's gourd: Mme Labrunie
A colossal wall map of Cairo: Francis Wey
An Arabian burnous: Henry Millot
A wedding chest, decorated with huntresses and satyrs: Sylvie
A bow and arrow from the Valois: Mlle Angélique de Longueval
A notebook of songs and music from the Valois: Mathilde Heine

And many things and many people besides. He asked that the blue cashmere shawl be sent to his mother in the Catholic cemetery in Gross-Glogau.

Leaving the café he saw that the contents of his room had vanished from the pavement. So his letter to Dr Blanche had been instantly effective. He felt an old pride in the power of the written word. His belongings having been dispersed as legacies to every loved one in his pantheon, now his way was clear—Place des Anglais, Rue Galande, to the Seine. He hurried. Not a soul on the Pont des Arts. What hour must it be then in this sleepless city? The river came towards him, engrossed by the freezing rains, crazy with flotsam and queer lights. These were the days and nights of his mother's death. He knew that behind his back dead soldiers of the Grande Armée were arriving from either bank, lying down, awaiting burial, the bridge was becoming heavy with them. He would not turn and look, he felt the cold of them on his back and the cold of the great river passing in silence beneath him. Now—he knew it—his mother began her crossing on an unsteady cart. She was feverous, she had been among the many dead, she had breathed their breath and was crossing now to her place of burial. He would not look, he stood in the river's draught and shook with cold as though his frame had no more covering than a skeleton's. He waited, bowed over the parapet, till his dying mother had gone by and the soldiers had vanished in the thin air.

Stéphanie Houssaye died 12 December of consumption. Nerval appeared at her funeral two days later in the Madeleine. It is not even certain he knew it was hers, not until he recognized friends among the mourners. He had taken to following any cortège he happened to encounter on the streets. He stood at several opened graves. Mourning with strangers for a stranger had become a part of his expiation. Strictly speaking, there *were* no strangers. But learning whose funeral he was attending in the Madeleine, he felt a profound grief, and further pains of conscience. Mme Houssaye had kept a room for him and he had disappointed her. He stood in a side chapel, looking on. Come in off the streets and now weeping helplessly, he was a spectacle. Nobody else showed such a helpless sorrow. His face was chapped, the tears made it look raw. As the service ended, he fled into another night already beginning.

He was seen in the Salon Littéraire, 67 Rue Sainte-Anne, on Christmas Day. Instalments of his work just finished and of things still under way were appearing in the journals. Early in January he appeared at the Odéon, at a performance of Dumas' *La Conscience*, between two strikingly beautiful women, said by some to be mother and daughter. He wore the black *redingote* and looked like a creature from elsewhere. He left abruptly during the second act, head down, mumbling excuses.

He spent entire days and sometimes the nights tramping the wastelands between the *faubourgs* and the gates of Paris. Alfred Delvau, author of *Histoire anecdotique des cafés et cabarets de Paris* (Dentu, 1862), records that one night in the Cabaret de la Canne, himself the only visitor, on the city's rim, by the abattoir, between the Barrière Rochechouart and the Barrière des Martyrs, Nerval came in, his thin black jacket caped with snow. The two men, not exchanging names, talked for hours. Delvau wrote up the encounter afterwards, by then, of course, knowing who the stranger was. He remembered his courtesy, the grace of his gestures, his chapped hands, his perfectly formed sentences ('fit to be written down'), the snow melting, and at length a faint steam rising, from his clothes. They swapped stories of the vilest places in Paris they had ever drunk, eaten, slept and been entertained in. Also, they imagined the afterlife. If there must be one, said Nerval, let the soul in it still have something to strive for. But frankly, he added, some nights I pray there will be none. He had known such happiness, he said, he had such memories of the sweetness of life, it would be a torment to him as a shade. Then he bowed, shook my hand, and made his exit into the still heavily falling snow.

3

He wrote: I was author and hero of my own novel. The gods were reading me. They watched with interest to see what I would make of myself. To which, with some asperity, one of his actresses replied: You were good at situations and at plots and sub-plots, one thing leading to another. But you were quite hopeless at dénouements. When did you ever bring anything to a conclusion? You were all beginnings and little forays hither and thither. That's what you enjoyed and that's what you were good at: inventing situations full of possibilities. To be absolutely honest, I doubt if they were watching you from Olympus. Gods and goddesses love endings, in my experience. And the bloodier the better, I might add.

In his head ('everything is in my head') he continued this conversation as he hurried with apparent purpose down one street or another or, through the *terrains vagues*, orbited the city's knotted heart. In truth, it was no conversation. One woman after another rose up and told him straight he was no good at endings. Dearest friend, you have a morbid horror of dénouements! He concurred. Every woman he had ever loved—and they were legion—had been right about him whether at the time they had delivered their verdict or not. Few had, in fact. They loved him too much. Even now in the cold, beyond the *faubourgs*, on the new boulevards, in the ancient fetid alleys, among the ruins and the sparkling new temples of commerce, where he passed, they followed, accusing him. He was a fleeing comet, they were the Furies on his tail. What nonsense! He sat in a draughty mausoleum in Père Lachaise, he summoned them up, he whistled them out of the north, south, east and west, some out of their early graves. And he gave them their parts, he wrote their lines, he coached them in their delivery, so that it would be irrefutably clear what his life-fault was and he would see once and for all what a mountain of amends he had to make.

He walked out to the Barrière de Pantin, which is an exit into the Valois. Should he or shouldn't he, for the old virtue of those places? He could not. He was weary, he was cold and weary to death. He turned without volition and let the lodestone of innermost Paris pull him in.

He found himself in Montmartre, Rue de l'Abreuvoir. It had stopped snowing, under a slant moon and more and more stars he halted in familiar whereabouts. Close by was the city's one surviving vineyard. The vines will survive the deep cold, they bide their time; when the year turns, they put out feelers, they bud, they leaf, they fruit. Silence. Stillness. Before long the cattle and the horses will come down the cobbled lane to the trough hereby and drink. The secret gardens will overflow their walls. There will be festivals on the homely streets, games and dancing and singing, joyous solemnities. Oh this *quartier*, oh this village above the city!

Very faintly, he heard one of the small hours striking. He walked around the walls of the house and garden of the Folie Sandrin, to the front gate, Rue Norvins. He might pull at the bell for ever and no night-attendant would open to him. It was long ago, and besides the doctor himself was dead. But oh, the gardens of that place, the abundant flowers, the gracious trees, the eternally self-replenishing fountains! He thought of them as lost to him, of himself as shut out from them, and his heart raced with gratitude to the father and his people gone from there and to the son and his people still in Passy, makers and custodians of asylum, physicians, ministers to minds diseased. What pain his antic disposition had dealt them and would deal them!

In childhood, motherless, he had been ripped from the Valois into the city. Time and again he went back there, by coach, omnibus, railway train and on foot, again and again, ever more in love, ever more ('petit Parisien') debarred. He slept in her woods, haunted her waters, forfeiting her, by neglect and failure, by growing up, until she was lost to him and thereafter, in one lodging and another, he must write about her. In which, now, trudging through the snow in leaky shoes around the *maison de santé* of the late Dr Blanche, he felt the breath, almost the shaping up, of some consolation. In a consciousness almost without name or particular identity, he rejoiced in the sleeping idyll of Montmartre and in the magical moon- and stars- and sun-lit domain of childhood in the Valois. His hands were too cold to search his pockets for the pen and any scrap of unscribbled paper, but he felt the sentence to be safe and sound: Reasons for joy, whether I live or die, are the asylum gardens, my doctors, father and son, and my constant returns to the country of my heart, my *knowledge* of it, cognizance through the feet and all the senses, love, love, my love.

This is the *rallentando* before the hurry to the end.

Like many an insomniac in the sleepless city he wandered till he found a café still open or just opening, sat himself down near the stove and ordered a grog. When his hands were warm enough, when they came back to life and would *work*, he retrieved from an innermost pocket a couple of sheets on which he had composed a prospectus for his *Complete Works*. Looking over it gave him great satisfaction, the scores of titles, nearly thirty years of publication. He added a few more 'subjects', some half-finished, some never begun but burning like super-novae in his head, and among these the Queen of Sheba whom he thought of as his own, he knew her, he could write her out, page after page, whenever he pleased. He laid his head on his arms and slept, warm. The *patron* let him be. When he woke, the place was busy with men taking a drink on their way to the day's hard labour. They saluted him, so he felt, as one of their kind, so that he blushed with pleasure, with a modest pride in himself, and returned their salutes. To complete the prospectus, he added, under the heading *Reflections. Philosophy. Religion*: 2 vols of manuscripts. Then hurried away in the trodden snow to the Rue Notre-Dame-des-Champs, to M. Jacob, agent of the publisher Dutacq, who had promised to publish him 'entire', and to pay him well. Afterwards Jacob remembered him as, yes, quite mad, but never wittier, never in better humour.

In the remaining nights the cold worsened. During that of 23–24 January the police found him with his jacket undone (all the bulging inner pockets visible), outside the Madeleine, clinging to the railings and chanting a paean or supplication to the Great Goddess. Quite gently they forced his frozen fingers open and conveyed him in a carriage to their station at Châtelet. There he raved, and lifted up his voice again. They strapped him to a bedframe in a cell out of earshot. Next morning, apologetically, with great courtesy, he asked would they send a note to M. Henry

Millot, a childhood friend, 13 Rue du Départ, who would vouch for his identity and take him off their hands. They obliged. Early afternoon, very surprised (he had not seen the man in question for twenty years), Millot was brought to him, recognized him for who he was from the engraving by Eugène Gervais published in *Les Contemporains* the year before. Yes, he would take him home, he would look after him, it would be an honour.

We sat together in a café on the Rue de l'Hirondelle, said Millot afterwards. He drank a cognac and a glass of St Émilion, enquired most courteously after my wife and family, and did not seem very mad, only now and then rather abstracted. We had been there an hour or so—the lights were already lit outside—when he stood up, excused himself, approached the bar and was directed through into the back yard. That was the last I saw of him, disappearing as though for two minutes.

He had seen the face of the young soldier who had served in Africa and was now in Purgatory unable to eat or drink. How certain he was, and patient! This is my ordeal. I have to pass through it. He felt again the joy of seeing the young man's eyes come open, so strangely blue, oh such joy! He knew he was ill, and he saw no reason not to call the illness madness. And he knew that the fateful truth shone through the mask of madness, his truth, his fate, killing perhaps. Cowering away from it only augmented his self-contempt, which feeling drove him not to run from, but in search of, that very truth. In equal measure he longed for and dreaded the signs of an outcome. They were beginning to multiply, the markers, the pointers, faces, letterings, birds. How long still? Such a lot of wrong self he had to slough off before he could even say for certain: now the ending has begun.

In that final day and in that final night the needle of his soul swung helplessly through every degree for the lost north.

He ran to the morgue, a Greek temple in appearance, on the Quai du Marché-Neuf. It was warmer in there than on the streets, light and airy, and populous too, people of all conditions, native and tourists, some with their children, strolled in the hall, and through walls of glass viewed the naked dead of all ages and conditions on marble slabs. He asked an attendant for a sheet of notepaper and wrote to his aunt: Once I have triumphed, you will have your place on my Olympus as I have my place in your house. He added that she should not expect him home for supper 'because the night will be black and white'. Leaving, he saw a barge mooring. He waited, though he knew what it meant. The drowned arrive by boat. Pandora was lifted out and carried past him on a stretcher. She drifted, singing, said the bearers. You'd never believe it, the weight of her now. He ran to the Pont Notre-Dame, working his ring loose, and—propitiation, harbinger?—flung it where the girl had come from. Flash of light. Nothing.

He remembered that three or four years ago he had received payment from Heinrich Heine to translate more of his poems into French. The work was unfinished, the advance never paid back. He began to run towards the Rue d'Amsterdam. He had no money to repay the debt, nor could he promise to complete the commission, all he could do was beg forgiveness. What number of such failures debars you even from Purgatory? He hurried, as though the clock would strike: too late! But at the fellow-poet's door he turned away. Had he not, on precisely the same heave of conscience, made precisely the same foot-journey during an earlier sojourn in the Underworld little more than a year ago? Repetition, eternal repetitions, a very simple machine, very few possible actions, round and round, again and again and again.

He was weary to death. He remembered a priest who had told him of another priest whose particular gift was the swaling away of madness with his waxen hands. His name was Abbé Dubois and he had his parish somewhere in Gentilly. He set off in that direction, rolling his shoulders, perhaps to propel himself more forcefully through the flurries of snow.

As though in a dream (a dreamer dreams he wakes), he found himself in a curiosity shop in the Rue de Valois, stock-still, merely waiting. He turned, clockwise, very slowly, searching, and soon saw what he did not know he was looking for. Only then did he notice the proprietor observing him. The very thing, sir. It belonged to the Queen of Sheba. I have a certificate saying so. Not expensive, said Nerval, making the purchase.

He crossed the river with no thought of drowning. He saw the Abbé Dubois' white hands, felt them on his burning head. But in the Rue de la Reine-Blanche, nowhere near Gentilly, all the virtue went out of him and he entered a café where an old woman was singing to a sick child and a ragpicker was reading the tarot. Nerval looked over his shoulder. Happy man, he said. Ordered wine for the woman, the ragman and himself. Sat apart by the stove and fell asleep. When he woke, the child and the ragman were both sleeping. The woman smiled at him. He drank off his wine, bowed to her and the *patron*, and in no hurry now began the return into the heart of Paris, to a street that while he slept had surfaced from the back of his mind.

4

From behind the ruins of Châtelet prison, leaving the slaughterhouse and carrying its blood and offal, the Rue Pied-de-Boeuf after forty yards or so joined the Rue de la Boucherie which itself, running parallel to the Seine, narrowing, darkening and descending, entered the Rue de la Vieille Lanterne. Lover of beauty, it was to that corner, in the zone of the dungeons, torture-chambers and places of execution, of the abattoirs and tanneries and of the gutters and sewers by which they passed their slops into the river, that in the night of 26 January 1855 Nerval walked through the dirty snow to die. People lived in that underworld, they had their being, went about their business, through slits they saw the sky or, on their level, the river bearing away the ordures and the drowned. He had been down there before, often, as though to assure himself that a place existed in which his nightmares and his horrors would always feel at home. That world, that real world of the city's streets. This street dropped lower by a flight of a dozen steps. Here there was a public baths (only think of its waters), a locksmith under the sign of a large key, and a lodging house under the sign of a lantern. Seven steps down was a landing, just to the left of which a sewer spilled out through a grille from the Marché Saint-Jacques. The locksmith had a pet raven, it perched on the key, and uttered the words *J'ai soif!* again and again. Dr Blanche said afterwards: he saw his madness face to face. He went where he would see it, on a date (twice thirteen) that fitted because it was doubly ill-omened. The crow said: Your gift has left you, you will thirst for ever. There were five further steps, to the very floor. There he found a stone, placed it on the bottom step, climbed up on it and threaded a cord which he believed had laced the stays of the Queen of Sheba, around the third bar of the sewer-grille; and of the two ends he made a noose. Against the cold—which had dropped to eighteen below—he was wearing everything he owned: the black *redingote*, two calico shirts, two flannel waist-coats, grey cloth trousers, patent leather shoes, reddish-brown cotton socks, a black collar, his black collapsible top hat. In his pockets were scraps of his writings, his old passport to the Orient and a white handkerchief. The day was beginning its efforts to get light, hopeless down there, on the floor, between cakey walls, under the locksmith's thirsty raven. He took off his hat, fitted the noose, firmly replaced his hat. Then kicked the stone away, swung out and tolled there, choking, his feet only a couple of inches above a resting place. When they found him, just before six, in that cold, he was still warm and his right hand was still moving. They bled him, uselessly. They carried him over the Pont au Change, displayed him on the marble in the morgue and sent for Gautier to come and identify him.

That same year the Rue de la Vieille Lanterne and all its foul connections, the leprous habitations, the cloaca, the slurried public square, the places of butchery and flaying, all were obliterated. It has been calculated that the grille he hung from in his comical hat was just below the curtain of the present Théâtre de la Ville (formerly Théâtre Sarah-Bernhardt)—in fact, exactly below where the prompter sits and helps the actors and actresses in their nightly comedies and tragedies, when they forget their lines.

Notes on the Stories

Introduction

Dans la rue des blancs manteaux
Le bourreau s'est levé tôt…

In the Street of the White Robes / The executioner rose early…

Le vieux Paris n'est plus (la forme d'une ville
Change plus vite, hélas! que le cœur d'un mortel)…

The old Paris is gone (the shape of a city / Changes more quickly, alas! than the heart of a man)…

Le Lapin Agile: A famous cabaret in the Rue des Saules frequented by many artists.

[1]

He branched off into the Rue Marie-Stuart, which was in fierce competition with Rue Brisemiche in the old days when it was called, more prosaically, Passage Tire-Vit and, later, Tire-Boudin: 'Pull-Penis' and 'Pull-Sausage'. The Rue Marie-Stuart was formerly known for its prostitutes, like the Rue Brisemiche in the 4th *arrondissement*.

[2]

Carte de Tendre: The *Carte de Tendre* or the *Carte du Tendre* (1653–4) of Madame de Scudéry was the name given to the map of the imaginary land representing the path to love according to the *précieuses*—the witty, intellectual women of the time.

chouans: French royalists in revolt against the Revolution.

[3]

Monsieur Delaunay: Probably Louis Arsène Delaunay, nineteenth-century French actor.

[4]

From *Le Journal*, 28 juillet 1901, collected in *Chez l'illustre écrivain*, and from *Contes cruels*, vol. 2 (Flammarion, 1919).

Saint-Lazare: Saint-Lazare was a women's prison in the nineteenth century.

Millerand: Alexandre Millerand, the Socialist President of France from 1920 to 1924.

[6]

Quai Saint-Paul: Now the Quai des Célestins.

chassepot barrels: A chassepot was a bolt-action breech-loading rifle.

the device: A small trumpet or mouthpiece.

2 December 1851: The date of the coup which brought Louis-Napoléon to power.

the *Cabinet Noir*: The *Cabinet Noir* was the office, later called the *Cabinet des Secrets des Postes*, where letters of suspect persons were opened and read by public officials before being forwarded to the addressees. The statesmen mentioned in the text served under Napoléon III.

Monsieur Piétri: Prefect Piétri was in charge of Louis-Napoléon's secret police.

Prince Pierre: 1845–1919. He was the grandson of King Louis Philippe I.

[7]
Landru: Henri-Désiré Landru (1869–1922) was a serial killer.

[9]
***salaud*:** A person who lives in bad faith, in the sense meant by Existentialists such as Sartre.

Mitterrand: François Mitterrand, President of France 1981–95.

CFDT: French trade union.

[13]

built formerly in Moret for Diane de Poitiers: Moret-sur-Loing in the department of Seine-et-Marne. Diane de Poitiers (1499–1566) was a famous court beauty and mistress of Henri II.

le Train Bleu: The luxury night express train to the Mediterranean that ran from 1886 to 2003.

merveilleuses: Members of a fashionable aristocratic subculture during the Directory, 1795–9.

Father Victory: Georges Clemenceau, who led the nation in World War I, was known as 'Père-la-Victoire'.

gentle Lolo, who became Boronali, whose picture I had exhibited at the *Salon des Indépendants* on the Cours-la-Reine: Dorgelès played a joke on the artists of the time by exhibiting a painting at the *Salon des Indépendants* in 1910 named 'Sunset over the Adriatic' which was, in fact, painted by the tail of a donkey named Lolo.

[16]

Cœur d'enfant, cœur d'enfant, que tu me fais de la peine!: Childish heart, oh my childish heart, what sorrow you cause me! I have been unable to find the origin of this quotation.

Bataille: Georges Bataille, writer, 1897–1962.

[17]

Lépine: Louis Lépine was Prefect of Police from 1893 to 1897 and from 1899 to 1913. He was particularly skilled at handling crowds.

[19]

Aux quatre coins du lit / Des bouquets de pervenches / Et nous y dormirons / Jusqu'à la fin du monde...: At each of the corners of the bed / Bunches of periwinkle / And we'll sleep there / Till the end of the world...

Notes on the Authors

Marcel Aymé (1902–67), a prolific novelist, short-story writer and dramatist, has a square named after him in Montmartre. In the middle is a statue depicting 'Le Passe-Muraille' ('The Man who Walked through Walls'), one of his most famous short stories.

Arnaud Baignot is a writer and translator formerly living in Paris. He specializes in the genre of the short story and is currently preparing a volume of stories with the theme of 'Doubles'.

Francis Carco (1886–1958), poet and novelist, was born in La Nouvelle-Calédonie, the French overseas territory in the South-West Pacific. He lived a bohemian life in Paris in the first years of the twentieth century, writing about it often in local Parisian dialect. He had an affair with the writer Katherine Mansfield in 1915 and is generally thought to be the narrator, Raoul Duquette, in her short story 'Je ne parle pas français'.

Colette, Sidonie-Gabrielle (1873–1954), writer and actress, born in a village in Burgundy, moved to Paris when she married. Apart from novels such as *Gigi* and the Claudine series, she wrote frequent sketches of life in Paris. She died in an apartment overlooking the Palais Royal gardens and was given a state burial in the Père Lachaise cemetery.

David Constantine, born 1944, is a poet and translator, novelist and short-story writer, and an Emeritus Fellow of the Queen's College, Oxford. The film *45 Years*, based on his story 'In Another Country', was released in 2015.

Didier Daeninckx, born 1949, is best known for his *romans noirs* and his short stories which have been widely translated and many of which are set in Paris. He has won the Prix Goncourt de la Nouvelle. Politically left-wing and a friend of journalists at *Charlie Hebdo*, he has told of his experience of treatment for a heart attack in a Paris hospital, when the surgeon, who had previously attended to one of the journalists from that newspaper, asked him to join in a minute's silence to remember the victims.

Roland Dorgelès (1885–1973) spent his childhood in Paris. He achieved fame with his novel about World War I, *Les Croix de bois*, which won the Prix Goncourt.

Frédéric H. Fajardie (1947–2008), author of more than thirty novels and screenplays, was a master of the 'new style of detective story'. A committed Marxist, his stories, like the one included here from *Nouvelles d'un siècle l'autre*, are full of violence and disillusion.

Aurélie Filippetti, born 1973, is a politician and novelist. She is a member of the Socialist Party and was Minister of Culture and Communication from 2012 to 2014.

Jean Follain (1903–71) was a poet and judge who won the Prix Blumenthal in 1941 for non-collaboration with the Vichy government. His poems have been widely anthologized. He died prematurely when he was run over in a car accident in Paris.

Julien Green (1900–98) was born of American parents in Paris and was brought up there. During the Occupation he lived in the United States.

Joris-Karl Huysmans (1848–1907) takes his name from his Dutch father. His early writing might be considered naturalistic, but with the publication of *Á rebours* in 1884 he came to be associated with the Decadent movement in French literature.

Guy de Maupassant, born near Dieppe in Normandy in 1850, is perhaps the most famous short-story writer in French literature. A protégé of Flaubert, he achieved instant fame with his story 'Boule de Suif' set in the Franco-Prussian war. His work has been translated into many languages. He died of syphilis at the early age of forty-two in 1893.

Octave Mirbeau (1848–1917) was a journalist, short-story writer, art critic, playwright and novelist who defied literary as well as social conventions. The story here is taken from his stories, *Contes cruels*, which were published in the press around 1900. He frequently alludes to contemporary events in his work and his novel *Journal d'une femme de chambre* was made into a film by Buñuel in 1964 and by Benoît Jacquot in 2015. Both films aim at (and succeed in) shocking the public.

Gisèle Prassinos, born 1920 in Istanbul, Turkey, emigrated with her family to France when she was two. She was discovered by the surrealist poet, André Breton, at the age of fourteen and published in the journal *Minotaure*. Her writing is characterized by the Surrealist movement's fascination with dreams and the unconscious.

Vincent Ravalec was born in Paris in 1962 and has always lived in or around the city. He left school at fourteen. His first collection of stories was published by *Le Dilettante*. He is well known for his films as well as for his writing, which includes novels, and stories for children.

Jacques Réda, poet and *flâneur*, was born in 1929 and lives and walks in Paris. His writing is largely about the streets of the capital. He was chief editor of the *Nouvelle Revue Française* for almost ten years.

Georges Simenon (1903–89) is the Belgian author of nearly 200 novels and short stories. Many of them feature the amiable Chief Inspector Maigret.

Émile Zola (1840–1902): his love of Paris is evident throughout his novels and short stories, in particular in his great *œuvre* the Rougon-Macquart series, twenty novels set in the Second Empire.

Selected Further Reading

On Paris

Paris, Guides Bleus (Harrap, 1991), a comprehensive guide to Paris, with a wealth of useful background information, detailed history, and maps.

Paris: The Secret History, by Andrew Hussey (Viking, 2006).

Dictionnaire Historique des Rues de Paris (2 vols.), ed. Jacques Hillairet (Les Éditions de Minuit, 1997). These two volumes contain detailed histories of each street and the buildings in them as well as photographs of streets in Paris in different decades.

Eugène Atget's Paris, by Andreas Krase, ed. Hans Christian Adam (Taschen, 2001). Photographic evidence of what Paris looked like in the first two decades of the twentieth century.

The Streets of Paris, by Richard Cobb, with photographs by Nicholas Breach (Duckworth, 1980). What Paris looked like in the last two decades of the twentieth century.

The Time Out Book of Paris Walks, ed. Andrew White (Penguin, 1999).

Two books on the evolution of Paris from Roman times to the present, both extremely well written and entertaining:

Seven Ages of Paris, Portrait of a City, by Alistair Horne (Macmillan, 2002).

Paris, Biography of a City, by Colin Jones (Penguin, 2004).

The Invention of Paris, by Eric Hazan, trans. David Fernbach. This book is subtitled 'A History in Footsteps' and is immensely lively and readable despite its 400 pages.

Anthologies of French Short Stories

The Oxford Book of French Short Stories, ed. Elizabeth Fallaize (OUP, 2002).

The Time Out Book of Paris Short Stories, ed. Nicholas Royle (Penguin, 1999). These are mainly by Anglophone writers.

XCiTés, ed. Georgia de Chamberet (Flamingo, 1999). A selection of stories and extracts from novels by twentieth-century French writers in the 1980s and 1990s.

French Short Stories, vols. 1 and 2, eds. Pamela Lyon and Simon Lee (Penguin, 1966 and 1972).

Short Stories in French, New Penguin Parallel Text, trans. and ed. Richard Coward (Penguin, 1999). These are bilingual texts and therefore useful for language students.

Comma Press has published several volumes of short stories, not only in French, that readers particularly interested in the relationship of stories and places may like. Consult their website for details of titles such as *ReBerth*, *Elsewhere*, and *Decapolis*, and their recent collections about Manchester, Liverpool, and Leeds.

Publisher's Acknowledgements

Marcel Aymé, 'Rue Saint-Sulpice', *Le Nain*, Gallimard, 1934

Arnaud Baignot, 'Rue de la Tacherie'

Francis Carco, 'Rue Pigalle', *Le Paris de M'sieur Francis*, Arcadia, 2005

Colette, 'Dans la foule', *Contes des mille et un matins*, Flammarion, 1970

David Constantine, 'Rue de la Vieille Lanterne'

Didier Daeninckx, 'Rue des Degrés', Éditions Verdier, 2010

Roland Dorgelès, 'Sur un toit des Champs-Élysées', *Regards sur Paris*, Éditions Bernard Grasset, 1968

Frédéric H. Fajardie, 'Cri de violeur, une nuit, à Montparnasse', *Nouvelles d'un siècle l'autre*, Librairie Arthème Fayard, 2005

Aurélie Filippetti, 'La Rue ne suffit pas', *Un toit, nouvelles sur le logement*, Cherche-midi, 2006

Jean Follain, 'Rues', *Paris*, Éditions Phébus, 2006

Julien Green, 'Cris perdus', *Paris*, Champ Vallon, 1983

Joris-Karl Huysmans, 'Rue de Chine', *À Paris*, Bartillat, 2005

Guy de Maupassant, 'Le Rendez-vous', *Contes et nouvelles*, Gallimard, 1979

Octave Mirbeau, 'Tableau parisien', *Contes cruels*

Gisèle Prassinos, 'L'Arbre aux trois branches', *Trouver sans chercher*, Flammarion, 1976

Vincent Ravalec, 'Le Pigeon taquin qui chiait sur la tête des gens', *La Vie moderne*, Éditions Le Dilettante, 1996

Jacques Réda, 'À pied ou à vélo', *La Liberté des rues*, Gallimard, 1997

Georges Simenon, 'L'Affaire du Boulevard Beaumarchais', *Les Nouvelles Enquêtes de Maigret*, Gallimard, 1944

Émile Zola, 'Vieilles ferrailles', *Contes et nouvelles*, 1865–72

Every effort has been made to trace and contact copyright holders prior to publication. If notified, the publisher will be pleased to rectify any omissions at the earliest opportunity.

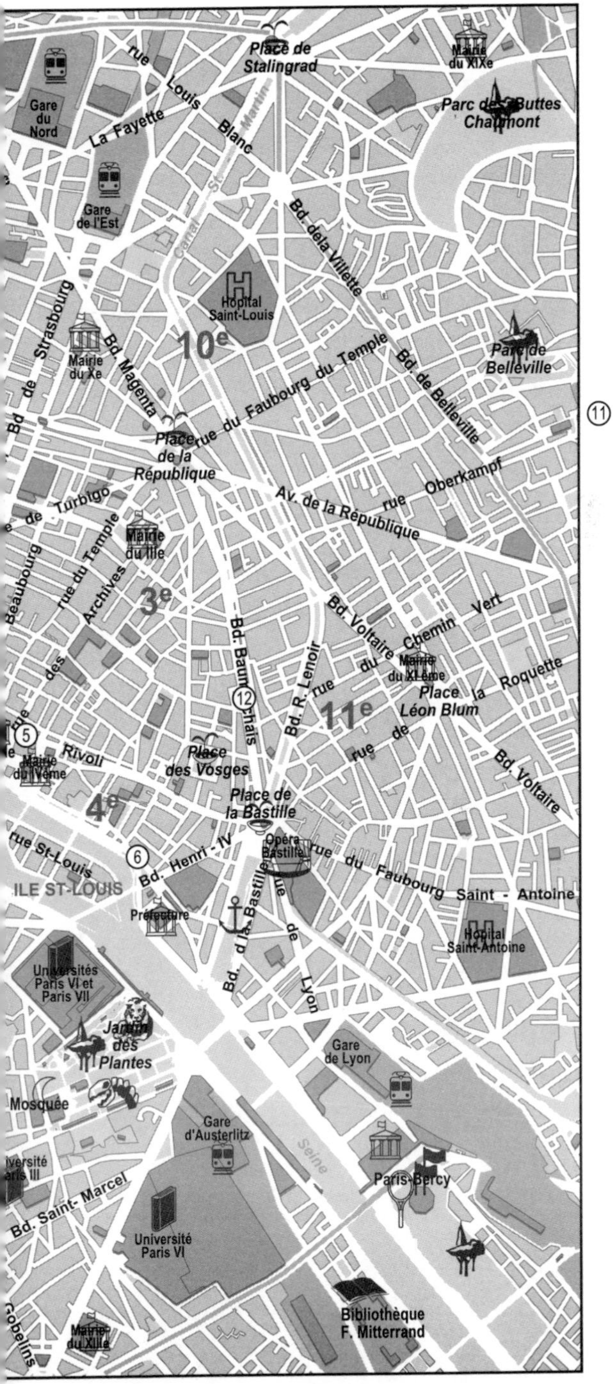
Place de Stalingrad
Mairie du XIXe
Parc des Buttes Chaumont
rue Louis Blanc
La Fayette
Gare du Nord
Gare de l'Est
Canal St-Martin
Bd. dela Villette
Hôpital Saint-Louis
10e
Bd de Strasbourg
Mairie du Xe
Bd. Magenta
rue du Faubourg du Temple
Bd. de Belleville
Parc de Belleville
11
Place de la République
rue Oberkampf
Av. de la République
rue de Turbigo
Mairie du IIIe
rue du Temple
Beaubourg
rue des Archives
3e
Bd. Beaumarchais
Bd. Voltaire
rue du Chemin Vert
Mairie du XIème
Bd. R. Lenoir
12
11e
Place Léon Blum
rue de la Roquette
5
Rivoli
Mairie du IVème
Place des Vosges
Bd. Voltaire
Place de la Bastille
4e
Opéra Bastille
rue St-Louis
6
Bd. Henri - IV
rue du Faubourg Saint - Antoine
ILE ST-LOUIS
Préfecture
Bd. de la Bastille
rue de Lyon
Hôpital Saint-Antoine
Universités Paris VI et Paris VII
Jardin des Plantes
Gare de Lyon
Mosquée
Gare d'Austerlitz
Seine
Université Paris III
Paris-Bercy
Bd. Saint- Marcel
Université Paris VI
Bibliothèque F. Mitterrand
Gobelins
Mairie du XIIIe